Angela
Llapktor

40 Pwlkswyddog
Thegaron

The Years Between

IRIS BROMIGE

The Years Between

Hodder & Stoughton

LONDON SYDNEY AUCKLAND TORONTO

British Library Cataloguing in Publication Data
Bromige, Iris
  The years between.
  I. Title
  823[F]

ISBN 0-340-40715-8

Published by Hodder and Stoughton,
a division of Hodder and Stoughton Ltd,
Mill Road, Dunton Green, Sevenoaks, Kent TN13 2YA
Editorial Office: 47 Bedford Square, London WC1B 3DP

Typeset by Hewer Text Composition Services, Edinburgh
Printed in Great Britain by Biddles Ltd, Guildford and King's Lynn

Contents

1

End of an Era

Nicholas Barbury emerged from a shadowy corner of the churchyard as the last of the mourners departed and sat on a wooden seat contemplating his grandmother's grave, piled high with flowers. The village church had been filled to overflowing, for Mirabel Rainwood had been a much loved and respected figure in the locality, and almost every member of her large family, covering four generations, had been present.

Returning to England after living for nine years in France, he was in no mood to meet his numerous relations with their probing questions. So the old lady had made her exit at last, in her ninety-sixth year. To the end, her mental vigour had remained unimpaired, but when he had come on a flying visit for her ninety-fifth birthday, her physical fragility had been such that he had been afraid to embrace her. And she, who shared his love of literature and, when they were alone together, matched his own pleasure in quoting from it, had on that occasion quoted to him, with a faint smile on her aristocratic old face:

> "How strange it seems, with so much gone
> Of life and love, to still live on!"

He was glad that she had died peacefully in her sleep in Bredon Lodge, the home that had been the focal point of the Rainwood clan, held together by the indomitable matriarch who ruled them all, to a greater or lesser extent, with love, firmness and compassion. He would have hated her to have finished her life in a hospital bed among professionally bright strangers – the fate, he thought wrily, of most in these institutionalised times.

It was peaceful in the churchyard, the only sound a robin's plaintive autumn song. A few yellow leaves drifted down from a silver birch tree nearby and came to rest like gold coins on the grass below. Mirabel Rainwood's death marked the end of an era for their clan. She had never forsaken the values of an earlier, more civilised age, nor lowered her standards of conduct to suit the fashionable permissiveness of recent decades. And, until the end, she had kept up her monthly tea-parties when as many members as possible of that large family were expected to turn up and thus keep in touch with her and each other. He, absent in France, had been the recipient of regular letters from her to the same end. He doubted whether the family would remain as closely in touch hereafter.

Now she slept in peace beside his grandfather, who had died five years ago. Theirs had been a very long and happy marriage, with Mirabel the dominant partner always, he suspected. His grandfather, lacking her insight into human nature, had never come to terms with the vast social changes of the post-war years. An honourable man, although that was almost a derisory term nowadays, grown intolerant with old age, but always stalwart in his support and care for his wife. And, for his grandparents, marriage vows were made for life, he thought bitterly, the thought of his own failed marriage rising like gall and bringing him to his feet.

With one last look at his grandmother's grave, he strode off to his car, the prospect of the family gathering at his cousin Robert's home a few miles away as inviting as the North Sea in January. After his long absence, with only infrequent and brief visits to England, and with the news of his divorce only recently made known to his sister and then, no doubt, conveyed swiftly along the family grapevine, he would doubtless be an object of some curiosity. There would certainly be more than one member of the Rainwood clan to say 'I told you so'. A private man, his relationship

2

with this octopus of a family had always been a mixture of affection and wariness, with a thread of dislike for one of the tentacles. He intended to make his reappearance brief.

Whatever his reservations, however, he was his usual cool, urbane self on joining the family party. Robert, the eldest of Mirabel Rainwood's grandchildren, and his wife, Bridget, greeted him with warmth.

"My dear Nick! Good to see you after all this time," said Robert. "A sad day. Can't believe the old lady's gone."

"We shall all miss her so much. It will never be the same again," said Bridget. "But come along and have a cup of tea, Nick. When did you arrive back?"

"Yesterday."

He followed her across the room, stationed himself behind what he considered a hideous potted palm, cup of tea in hand, and surveyed the Rainwood clan at full strength. He had forgotten the level of noise at these family gatherings. The members of the fourth generation he scarcely recognised after nine years, but registered the fact that Robert's awful child had been transformed into a seemingly civilised young man who was carrying round a tray of biscuits, and that a group of teenagers of both sexes in a huddle on the far side of the room sported an array of strange fashions which he could only regard with a pained expression. And why, he wondered, was that girl with the spiky hair wearing only one ear-ring that looked like an outsize brass curtain ring?

His eyes continued to rove round the room, coolly appraising. On the whole, his own generation, now into middle age, had worn pretty well. His Uncle Peter had become grossly fat, his Uncle Derek as thin as a bean-pole. His cogitations on the effects of time on the Rainwoods were broken into by his younger sister, Frances, who bore down on him with a warm smile.

"Nick! We weren't sure that you would be here. Why didn't you let us know? We could have put you up. Where are you staying?"

"At a hotel near Gatwick airport. You look well, Frankie. How are Rolf and the offspring?"

But Frankie was not to be diverted, and having given him

a brief and satisfactory report on the state of her family, she returned to his affairs.

"How long are you here for?"

"No definite plans yet."

"We were all so sorry to hear about you and Debbie."

"Yes. How long is this party going on, do you suppose?"

"Robert is laying on a cold supper. Grandma wouldn't want us to be miserable, but she'd be glad that we joined forces today to say goodbye to her. She was more than ready to go, you know."

"Yes."

"Do come and stay with us while you're here, Nick. We've missed you."

"Thanks, Frankie, but I'll be moving around, researching a new biography. Well, well, if it isn't Susan heading our way, not in a spirit of love for me, I fancy." said Nick, a little smile on his lips which boded ill for this cousin.

And while Frankie stood by, wincing, Nick parried Susan's barbed little remarks about the sad news of his divorce with the exquisite politeness which had been his grandmother's most telling weapon, finding the chinks in Susan's armour with silky skill.

"And how is Felix? Still immersed in work? And his daughter? Amanda has grown into a very attractive young woman. You must be proud of her."

And Susan, whose marriage to Felix had been under strain for years past, gave him a tight little smile and moved away.

"Claws," said Frankie indignantly.

"Spoilt silly by her father from the day she was born. I suppose it's hard for her to live with the knowledge that Felix, whom she stole from Bridget, has never ceased to regret his mistake. Everything showered on her, except the one thing she wanted: Felix's wholehearted devotion. All this marrying – a great mistake," he concluded drily.

"Not always."

"Heavens, what a din! Your husband seems to be trying to attract your attention, Frankie."

4

"Don't disappear, Nick. We've lots to talk about."

But disappear was just what he intended to do. Slipping through the throng, with a polite hail and farewell to various relatives on the way, he had just taken leave of Robert and Bridget when he was caught at the door by his elder sister, Jennifer.

"Nick, I've been trying to get to you, but I got pegged into a corner by Jonathan. Oh, what a bore that cousin is! Why on earth should he think I'd be interested in nuclear physics?"

"Our brilliant boffin needs an audience, dear, and you are too kind to repulse him."

"I know he has a remarkable brain, but he does seem so devoid of human feeling. He's not the least bit interested in any of us."

Nick smiled, saying:

> "For he has cut the human chain
> To kneel in worship to his brain."

"That's good."

"Not original. Someone else's words, slightly adapted. How are things up in Northumberland, Jenny?"

"Fine. Will you be here long enough to come and stay with us, Nick? It's years since you visited the Northumberland branches of the family. Joel would be so pleased, and Giles and Kit at Castleton. And you hardly know the young fry. Valerie is fifteen and I don't believe you've seen her more than twice in your life. She couldn't come with us because she's got an important exam at her college of music just now."

"She takes after you in that respect, then, Jenny. I know I'm very remiss, but my plans are a bit vague just now."

"Well, I know it's like trying to tie down an eel where you're concerned, but we're fond of you, Nick. Don't ever forget that," she said gently.

"And I don't deserve it," he said, looking at her with a softened expression. At forty-one, she might have been ten years younger. Hers was a sensitive face, framed with

5

smooth, fair hair, remarkable by virtue of the unexpectedly dark brown eyes and eyebrows that contrasted with her fair complexion. A quiet, gentle person, with a certain grace and self-possession which had always marked her out.

"I won't badger you, Nick. I know that there are times when the pressure of the family can be too much. There are so many of us. I remember I found it so once when I was deeply unhappy, and I escaped to the Border country. But it helps, sometimes, to have a complete change of scene. We wouldn't weigh heavily. Would leave you to yourself, if need be. No questions. Think about it, and come if it appeals. We'd be so happy to welcome you."

And with a gentle pressure on his arm, she left him. Nick, making his way to his car, reflected that Jenny, who had known deep unhappiness when she was young, had sensitive antennae for pain in others. He might think about her invitation. But first, there was one friend he *could* look forward to meeting the next day.

He arrived at Jean Brynton's cottage in Sussex on that still autumn morning earlier than he had arranged and, getting no response to his knock, walked round the side of the house and saw her at the far end of the garden, picking some chrysanthemums. He stood in the shadow of the cottage, watching her. It was five years since he had last seen her on a fleeting visit with Debbie, and had been shocked then at the change in her since her husband's death the year before. It was as though Darrel had taken all her vitality with him, leaving a gentle, resigned shadow of her old self. He hoped that time would have healed the loss, but when she straightened up and began to walk slowly back to the cottage, she seemed a stranger to him, a thin, middle-aged, frail-looking figure. How old was she now? Two years younger than he. Forty-one. Where had the years gone since they were all together in Ireland, he, Darrel, Jean and his young cousin, Tonie, in that golden summer?

Then she saw him, and her face lit up.

"Nick! Dear Nick! Oh, it *is* good to see you."

He put a friendly arm round her shoulder as the stranger vanished and it was the old Jean with the tawny brown eyes, toffee-coloured hair and sensitive mouth. With the bunch of golden chrysanthemums in her arms, she looked part of the autumn scene, but the shoulder he held was painfully thin.

If the old, easy relationship was still there as they talked over coffee of Mirabel Rainwood, of his writing, of her ten-year-old daughter, Diana, he was aware that they were skirting the matters that touched them most deeply, afraid of trespassing on sensitive ground.

It was while Jean was preparing a cold lunch for them that he noticed the two photographs on the bookcase, one of Darrel evidently taken in the garden with Diana perched on his shoulder, the other a group of Darrel and Jean, a couple whose names he had forgotten, and himself, looking unbelievably young.

"That holiday in Menton," he said, smiling as Jean came in carrying a bowl of salad. "Far away and long ago."

"Yes. I always liked that photograph of you. I thought we'd have a meal in here rather than in the dining-room, Nick, as you said you only wanted a snack. It's cosier in here, looking out on the garden."

"It looks as though it's more than a snack you've prepared, my dear," said Nick, eyeing the cold chicken, salad, Stilton cheese and a dish of pears. "And my favourite, Chablis, bless you."

Over lunch they still studiously avoided the personal in favour of impersonal topics, talking of books and music, both subjects of prime interest to them, until Jean said, as she sipped the last of her wine, "I wish you could stay longer and meet Diana. She'll not be home from school until four, though."

"My godchild. I get very nice thank-you letters from her at Christmas and birthday times."

"I've just had a photograph taken of her. I'm waiting to get a frame for it."

She fetched the photograph from a drawer in a bureau and Nick studied it. The dark-haired young girl in school

7

uniform looked back at him with a thoughtful expression on a face mature for a ten-year-old.

"She's like Darrel, isn't she? I wish I could stay and see her but I'm moving out of the Gatwick hotel this afternoon, off to London for a few days. Have to see my agent and publishers."

"When do you return to France?"

"I'm not returning. I sold the house and all its contents last month. At the moment, I've no definite plans. My sister, Jenny, wants me to go up to stay with the Northumberland limb of the family. Think I'll take her up on that, but only for a week or so. Too much family is apt to give me indigestion. But the Border country relatives are a nice bunch."

"It sounds a good idea," said Jean, taking the hint from his light tone. "Any new book lined up?"

"Yes. One about the Brownings in Italy. The early years have been thoroughly worked over but there's some unploughed material in those later years, I feel."

"You'll need a base for your work."

"Yes. A friend from my journalist days has just retired from journalism and bought a small hotel near Deanswood. He's willing to put a bedroom and sitting-room at my disposal – for the winter months, anyway. I'll probably dig in there. I should be able to work there without distraction, and as I'll be away a good deal researching in Italy, it will be pointless taking on any sort of permanent home."

"It will be good to have you close at hand, Nick, but I promise not to intrude."

"You never would, my dear." His eyes fell again on the photograph of Darrel and, after a moment's hesitation, he went on, "Jean, Darrel. Does it hurt to talk about him?"

"No. Especially not with you, Nick. You and he were good friends."

"It's been a hard time for you."

"Yes. Darrel wrapped a warm cloak round me. The world's seemed cold without him. But I've been helped by good friends. His successor at the Horticultural Station and his wife have been very kind to me. And there's Diana. And your letter helped. I've kept it, and read it many times

8

since. So I manage," she concluded cheerfully.

"Music must be a great consolation. You have a gift worth exercising there. I hope you haven't neglected it," he said, his eyes turning to the closed piano.

"I listen more than I play these days."

"Music and books. We'd do better to concentrate on them. Personal relationships are the devil."

"You and Debbie, Nick. I'm so sorry."

"Only myself to blame. I should have stuck to my old conviction that I was never made for the domestic cage. Now, if you'll forgive me for leaving you, my dear. We'll keep in touch."

She stood at the gate to wave him off. He took away an impression of a lonely, vulnerable woman, her personality somehow quenched. Time had dealt both of them some sickening blows. More fools them, he thought grimly, for falling in love and giving hostages to fortune. And as he accelerated after joining the main road, he said to himself, "Never again."

Jean, clearing away their lunch things, wondered just how Nick's marriage had broken up. It was obviously a 'No Entry' path. He had never been a man to reveal his feelings. Cool, assured, witty, an established writer and, until he met Debbie, a confirmed bachelor, this was the first failure in a singularly untroubled and successful life, and would doubtless have hit the harder for that. But he was not going to enlighten her, and she could only feel saddened at this misfortune, for she was fond of Nick, and their friendship stretched back many years. Debbie was a sweet-natured girl, and Nick a delightful companion. She could not guess what had gone wrong. Her only reservation about their marriage had been that Debbie, nine years his junior and, at that, a little immature for her age, had been too young for him.

She picked up the photograph of their holiday group again. Nick, a fair Adonis, wore that cool, faintly sceptical little smile she knew so well. They all looked so happy and young. Her thoughts went even further back to that wonderful holiday in Ireland when she had first met

Nick and his young cousin, Tonie, and had fallen in love
with Darrel. A beautiful country, unexpectedly sunny
weather, love, misunderstandings, but so much laughter and
happiness as well. A golden summer. Another world. Another
time. "Never glad confident morning again."

Unsettled, old memories disturbed by Nick's visit, she
sought sanctuary in the garden, attacking the weeds invad-
ing the rose bed.

2

Emma Vurney

"Nick," said Jennifer a little warily, "how long do you think you'll be staying at this hotel in Sussex?"

"Can't say. It'll be my base for the winter months, anyway, when I'm not in Italy researching for my next book. Foresters looks very pleasing from here, Jenny. Fits into the landscape as though they evolved together."

They had climbed the hill behind the house to a stretch of moorland. The wooded valley below was a tapestry of soft colours in the late autumn sunshine and the grey stone gables of Foresters were visible above the trees on the rising ground beyond.

Jennifer shot a sidelong glance at her brother. Always elegantly clad, even the casual country clothes of grey tweed trousers and polo neck grey sweater sat on him with a sophistication at odds with this rugged Border country. With his slim figure and fair classical looks, his forty-three years sat lightly on him. She decided on a cautious tactical approach.

"I'm so glad you came, Nick. We've missed you all these years. And just in time to share in the celebration of my niece's twenty-first birthday with the rest of us. You'll like Emma. Everybody does."

"That's a large claim, Jenny. Family gatherings have never been high on my list of pleasures, you know."

"I'm not talking of the whole Rainwood clan, only the Northumbrian branch you've always neglected."

"Northern climate too harsh for me, dear."

"Oh Nick! We don't live in the arctic circle, you know. Just clean bracing air here. Good for you."

"Ominous words. It's been good for you, anyway, Jenny. Isn't Emma the child you looked after when you first came up here?"

"Yes. The daughter of Joel's brother, Alan. I looked after her for a year while her parents were in India and Joel was landed with her and an invalid mother. She's as dear to me as my own daughter. A handful, though. Then and now."

Nick, studying the landscape, made no comment and appeared little interested in the subject of Emma. Jennifer, undeterred, went on, "She's just finished her three-year physical training course and is about to go into partnership with a friend in running a riding school in Sussex."

"She hardly needed three years' training for that."

"Not what her parents expected, or would have chosen, but Emma has her own very decided views. Her friend Lucy has spent all her spare time helping out at these stables ever since she was a schoolgirl, it seems. The stables are in Deanswood in Sussex, near her home. The owner of the stables, an eccentric old boy, took a great liking to Lucy and, when he died of a heart attack last June, she found to her amazement that he'd left the whole outfit to her."

"Really? Sounds rather a crazy enterprise for your Emma to embark on."

"She's always loved riding and anything to do with horses."

Nick appeared to find more interest in the landscape than in the subject of Emma and horses, and merely said cryptically, "It takes all sorts. How far is this castle you want to show me, Jenny? It's not that smudge on the horizon, is it?"

"It's only two or three miles."

"Too far," said Nick, decidedly. "I'll drive you there some time."

"You soft artistic types!" said Jennifer, shaking her head. "We'll walk as far as the bridge down there, then, and walk

12

back along the river. You're staying at a hotel in that part
of Sussex, aren't you, Nick?"

"What part of Sussex?" he asked blandly.

"Deanswood."

"A mile or two away, yes."

"I know it's only going to be your base and you expect
to be travelling a good deal of the time, but I wonder if
you'd be kind enough to keep an eye on Emma for us?"

Nick eyed his sister with astonishment.

"Keep an eye on a twenty-one-year-old? You must be
joking. This is the nineteen nineties, you know, not the
Victorian era. I've no doubt the young woman in question
could teach me a thing or two."

"It's a simpler life we lead up here, Nick. Emma is a
very unsophisticated girl. Warm-hearted, impetuous, could
easily be taken in. She's never been far away from home.
We're a bit anxious about her being cut off, knowing nobody
in those parts. If she just had someone responsible to turn
to, we'd feel happier."

"Nothing doing, my dear. I'm sorry. But I've a book to
write, I want no distractions and the last rôle I'd choose
to play is that of watchdog to any young woman. And it
would be the last thing Emma would want, I'm sure."

"Not a watchdog. Just taking an interest. Seeing that
she finds suitable lodgings. She hasn't a clue where she's
going to live. Thinks blithely that she'll find somewhere on
the day she arrives. Perhaps you could scout around a bit
before then."

Nick lifted his arms in a gesture of despair.

"I might have known! The Rainwood clan always used
me as the family handy-man until I married and went out
of reach. Best man, godfather, trouble-shooter, arbiter. And
never was anybody less suited to the rôle. Now, no sooner
am I back in England after nine years abroad than I'm
roped in again. No, Jenny. I refuse to get involved in
family affairs. My work needs all my concentration, and
the idea of keeping an eye on some happy-go-lucky horsey
girl is ludicrous. Good grief! Girls lead independent lives
from their early teens these days. You're out of touch,

my dear. I bet Emma would laugh her head off at the idea."

"She could be a happy distraction for you, Nick. She was for me at a time when I was very unhappy. She's so full of life."

"I am not drawn to young females who are full of life," said Nick, his slight drawl getting more pronounced, which was, Jennifer knew, a bad sign, and she pressed no more, hoping that when he met Emma he might feel differently. After all, her brother had always been a cool, detached observer of life, with reason always ruling his heart. So when this avowed bachelor had married Deborah Ryan, the whole Rainwood clan had been astonished and not averse to seeing him have to eat his words on the subject of matrimony. But Jennifer knew him to have a kind heart under that urbane exterior, and several members of the family had reason to be grateful to him for past help. She hoped that his failed marriage had not withered that kindness to leave him an unredeemable sceptic in middle age. She comforted herself with the thought that even the most deeply rooted scepticism might well be weakened by young Emma Vurney.

Nick's less than enthusiastic participation in the twenty-first birthday celebrations of Emma was masked by his customary cool charm, although the company of boisterous young people was not in tune with his taste or his mood of the moment. Irritated by his sister's efforts to involve him, he had no intention of allowing them to succeed and, after being introduced to Emma and congratulating her on the occasion, he had gracefully escaped to a remote corner of the crowded room, and, glass of champagne in hand, had shortly slipped away, with Alan Vurney's permission, to inspect the latter's library of travel books, of which he was an avid collector.

His first encounter with Emma had merely confirmed the ludicrous nature of Jennifer's suggestion, for this fair-haired girl with the speedwell blue eyes and lively manner exuded confidence and, to judge from the decided chin, a

14

determination to go her own way. Nothing doing, my dear sister, he thought as he entered the peaceful haven granted to him by Emma's father.

He was sitting on the arm of a chair, leafing through a book on the Himalayas, when Emma herself appeared.

"Oh, hullo," she said. "A refugee from the clans?"

"Guilty."

"Not to worry. I just came for an extra chair. We're putting on some charades."

Nick gave a gentle shudder. This was all too reminiscent of the Rainwood family parties of his youth. Emma regarded him with her head on one side, inclined to linger.

"You know, you're not a bit what I expected. When Auntie Jenny told me her brother was coming, the famous biographer, I expected a bearded, grave, elderly type."

"Really?" said Nick, a little startled at this directness.

"Mm. I expect you're awfully bored with my crowd. Not exactly an intellectual gathering."

"It would be an unusual twenty-first birthday party that was. I'm a renegade, I fear. I played truant from my own twenty-first birthday party many years ago, and was taken to task for it by my grandmother."

"Grandma Rainwood. I met her once when I was a tot, and she gave me an ivory horse-shoe for luck. I've still got it. She came up again to stay with Uncle Joel and Auntie Jenny when Valerie was christened. I liked her."

"Yes. She was a remarkable woman, my grandmother."

Emma leaned on the back of the chair she had chosen and regarded him with the assessing air of a judge at a dog show before saying, "I expect they've told you that I'm joining a friend in running a riding school in Sussex."

"Jenny did mention it, yes."

"Disapproval all round. I can't think why. Of course, they expected me to go in for teaching, but a chance to have one's own business is too good to miss, don't you think?"

"Depends on the business. I find it hard to imagine enjoying working with horses, but then the great outdoors has never been my scene," drawled Nick, intent on ruling out the rôle of ally.

"I like the freedom. Of being self-employed, I mean."

"An illusion. You take on the chains of responsibility."

"But you make the rules. I guess you've always opted for that. It must be grand to be a writer. We studied your book on the Victorian poets at college. I loved it."

"Well," said Nick, astonished, "I never imagined anything I wrote would play any part in physical education."

"We were able to take subsidiary courses at our college, and I chose literature."

Nick looked at her with rather more interest. Young Emma Vurney had some surprises for him, it seemed. Her eyes were as bright as a squirrel's as she met his gaze.

"And when are you joining this friend of yours?"

"I'd arranged with Lucy to leave here in two weeks' time. She's in Switzerland until then, staying with her grandmother. But I've decided to go to Deanswood next week and have a scout round for lodgings before Lucy gets back. She's invited me to stay at her home, but I don't want to do that. So I hope to get something fixed up quickly. I've booked a room at a small hotel in Deanswood for a couple of nights. Can't afford to stay long, though. I suppose you don't know anybody who lets rooms in that area? Auntie Jenny said you were staying near Deanswood for a time."

"I'm not familiar with the area and don't expect to be there long, but I've a friend who has lived there many years. She might be able to help. I'll give you her address and telephone number."

Emma took the details down on the pad on her father's desk and smiled her thanks, at which point a head came round the door and an indignant voice said, "What on earth are you doing, Emma? We've been waiting hours."

"Over to you," said Emma briefly, handing the chair to the tousled-haired boy who was regarding her with a far from friendly expression. Seizing the chair angrily, he left them without a glance at Nick, and Emma shrugged her shoulders.

"Horrible boy, my cousin Martin. Not really my cousin. Don't know what he is. Auntie Jenny's cousin Christine's son. What does that make him?"

"Very distant," said Nick, smiling. "Christine's twins, from what I've seen of them, have inherited some of the more regrettable Rainwood characteristics, but sixteen is an awkward age. Time for improvement."

"Simon's not so bad. Rather nice, in fact. But Martin!" Words failing Emma, she made for the door. "I must get things organised. It's nice knowing you, Uncle Nick. You don't seem like an uncle, though. Perhaps . . . Nick? I'm sorry I shan't be choosing my best mount for you at our riding school."

And she was gone, leaving Nick to reflect that preconceived notions about each other had proved surprisingly wrong to both parties. He would telephone Jean in the morning to prepare her. Meanwhile, he was finding Alan Vurney's library very rewarding. As so often in his life, he took refuge in books.

3

Setback

Emma found Jean Brynton a sympathetic listener as she poured out her hopes for the riding school.

"I'd like to explore the possibility of helping handicapped children to ride. A sort of therapy. It must be awful not to be mobile. Do you ride?"

"Not now. When I was young I ventured now and again. My daughter, Diana, takes to it."

"How old is she?"

"Ten."

"Best to start young. I had my first pony when I was five. I love riding. But then we have fine country for riding in Northumberland. Of course, the South Downs are lovely, too," added Emma tactfully.

"Is your friend an equally experienced rider?"

"Oh yes. She's spent all her spare time at these stables ever since she was a schoolgirl, and then the old Colonel left the whole business to her. Wasn't that an amazing slice of luck? He was very fond of Lucy, but she never dreamed of anything like this."

Jean, who had no particular liking for horses and would have viewed a legacy of riding stables with something akin to horror, turned the conversation to the urgent matter of accommodation.

"I made some enquiries about lodgings for you after Nick telephoned me, but I've drawn blank so far. If you're really stuck, though, I can put you up temporarily while you have a look round. That is if you don't mind an attic bedroom."

"Oh, that *is* kind of you. I can't afford to stay in this hotel after this week. Of course, it must be a business arrangement."

"Be my guest for a week or two. Something will turn up, I'm sure. Worth looking at the advertisements in the village newsagent's window."

"I'll do that. I'm really very grateful."

"What about your friend, Lucy? Hasn't she any ideas?"

"She's on holiday in Switzerland at the moment. She doesn't expect me down here for another fortnight, when she'll be back. As a matter of fact, she suggested I lodge at her home, but I don't want to do that. I thought if I came here ahead and could get fixed up before Lucy gets back, it would save me the embarrassment of refusing Lucy's offer with no good reason for doing so. You see," added Emma, noting the quizzical expression on Jean Brynton's face, "Lucy lives with her brother and his housekeeper in a house on the outskirts of Dilford. And I don't get on with the brother. I couldn't possibly live under the same roof."

Emma's lips had tightened and her eyes sparkled. How young she is, thought Jean. Young, and so vividly alive.

"He thinks I'm a bad influence on Lucy," added Emma grimly.

"I find that quite absurd."

"Me, too. That's why I'm so keen to make a success of our enterprise. Philip was dead against it. I'm going to prove him wrong."

"Good luck. My money is on you."

"It's Lucy's misfortune, having a brother like that. He dominates her. That's why he dislikes me. I encourage Lucy to be independent, do her own thing. She's such a kind, good-natured person, she can't bear to cross swords with anyone. Fortunately, being in college and away from home for three years has given her a taste for freedom."

"What about her parents?"

"They were both killed in a road accident when Lucy was only fifteen. Lucy was with them. She escaped with only minor injuries but went through a bad time, and Philip,

19

who lived in a flat in Dilford then, returned to the home he'd inherited, installed a housekeeper and took charge of Lucy. I think it's time he realised that his sister can stand on her own feet now."

"Does he work locally, this tyrant?" asked Jean, amused by Emma's fierce attitude.

"In Dilford. He's an osteopath. Fixes people's bones and all that. And he thinks he can fix Lucy's life, too, it seems."

"I think I know him. Would it be Philip Rogart?"

"Yes."

"I took Diana to his surgery a year or so ago, after she'd injured her back. My doctor referred me to him, and he put matters right for Diana with half a dozen sessions."

"Oh, I expect he's good at his job," said Emma, shrugging. "Efficiency written all over him. Didn't you find him insufferably arrogant?"

"Well, it wasn't a social encounter. Strictly professional. As a matter of fact, I rather liked him. At least, I felt that Diana was in good hands. And so it proved, because she had no more trouble, and prior to that she'd had all sorts of investigations and treatments which had got nowhere. One must give the devil his due," she concluded with a smile.

"It's nice here," said Emma, changing the subject as she put down her cup of coffee and looked out of the window at the garden, still colourful in the late autumn sunshine, with a carpet of gold and russet leaves spread across the grass, and some peach-coloured chrysanthemums lighting up the far corner. "I'm most awfully grateful to you for offering to put me up. I hope I'll not be a burden for long."

"You won't be a burden, Emma. But you'd better come upstairs to see your room before you commit yourself."

"Oh, I know I shall be happy here. I must thank Uncle Nick for putting us in touch. He doesn't seem an uncle, does he? I suggested dropping the title, but I sensed that he didn't altogether approve."

"Nick is a bit of a stickler for the niceties."

"I think he's a gem. All that charm, good looks and a

20

famous writer, too. He bowled me over," concluded Emma ingenuously.

"I'm not surprised."

"I mustn't take up any more of your time with my babblings. I'll move in at the end of the week, then, and thank you again for coming to my rescue. Now, I want to go to the stables and have a good reconnoitre. I've only seen them once, when I spent part of the vacation with Lucy last spring and we went riding."

"Won't you come up and see your room?"

"Not to worry. I know I shall like it here," said Emma, giving Jean a beaming smile and taking her leave.

Happy at this piece of good fortune, for she had taken a liking to Jean Brynton, and looking forward with growing excitement to examining the riding school and stables which offered such an inviting challenge to herself and to Lucy, Emma sped off on her hired bicycle along lanes festooned with the silvery-grey seed-heads of wild clematis swarming over bare trees and bushes, avoiding fallen conkers and drifts of leaves with gay abandon.

She rather hoped that Jim Brushford, who had been the Colonel's right-hand man and who had agreed to stay on for six months while she and Lucy got to grips with the business, would be occupied so that she could look round on her own before discussing it further with him and then have a session in the office with Jim's wife, who dealt with the administrative and book-keeping side.

At the entrance to the premises she was brought to a halt, for a newly painted board bore the words: *The Brushford Riding School*. Puzzled, she was trying to work this out when Jim Brushford himself came down the drive riding a bay mare.

"Hullo, Mr Brushford. You don't remember me? I'm Emma Vurney. I met you last spring when Lucy Rogart and I hired horses here. I'm her partner," added Emma, a little put out by his lack of recognition.

"Oh, yes," he said blankly.

He was a thin-faced, wiry looking man, with a weather-beaten complexion, well turned out in hacking jacket and breeches.

"I was wondering whether you'd be kind enough to show me round, and put me in the picture, before Lucy and I take over."

"Take over what?"

"Why, this riding school that Lucy inherited from the Colonel."

"I'm afraid the lines of communication have got crossed. I own this business now. Miss Rogart sold it to me a few weeks ago. Didn't she tell you?" he added, seeing the amazement on Emma's face.

"No. I can't believe it. We had it all worked out."

"I'm sorry."

"But . . . but she'd never do this without discussing it with me."

He shrugged and the mare moved restlessly.

"You'd better ask her brother. He was in on the negotiations. Miss Rogart is away in Switzerland, I believe. She was leaving a few days after we signed the deeds. Now, if you'll excuse me . . ."

"Mr Brushford," she said as he moved off. "Would you want an assistant? I'm an experienced rider."

"Sorry. We're fully staffed. Good morning to you," he said, touching his hat and moving off down the lane.

Aghast at this complete reversal of her plans, Emma cycled back to the hotel with her thoughts in such a whirl that she was nearly run down by a tradesman's van when she turned into a wider lane without due care. Sick with disappointment, she guessed who was responsible for this backing down by Lucy. Philip Rogart. He had never approved of her or the project. But Lucy had known that all along. Why back down at this late stage, and without letting her know? It was not in Lucy's nature to be so ruthlessly inconsiderate. Hurt and amazed at this blow from her closest friend, she viewed her situation grimly. Landed here, with little money and no job, she was faced with having to return home ignominiously after fighting her parents for the right to strike out on her own, for they had more or less shared Philip Rogart's views.

A little of the hurt and bewilderment was eased, however,

when she reached the hotel and found a package awaiting her. It had been readdressed to her by her mother. Inside was her copy of *Huckleberry Finn* and a letter from Lucy.

Dear Emma,

Don't know how to tell you this, but I've decided to sell the riding school, after all. Talking it over with Philip and Jim Brushford, I feel that we'd be taking on more than we could chew.

I know you'll be terribly disappointed, which is why I've been delaying letting you know. I hate letting you down when you'd set your heart on it, but this will reach you before you leave home, so no harm done, and you'll be able to look round for a job in your own Border country, which you love. Perhaps it's all for the best.

I'm just off to Interlaken for my holiday with Grandma. Hope to do some modest climbing, and when ferreting out my gear, I found your Mark Twain book, after searching high and low before we left college. How it got in that old hold-all, I shall never know. Anyway, here it is. Afraid I'm not on Mark Twain's wavelength. I did try!

Am putting aside the problem of getting a job until after my holiday, but I can't say I'm drawn to teaching after my practical trial at that awful school last term. Don't think I'm good at ordering people about! But what else besides P.E. am I trained for? Perhaps physiotherapy?

Hope you won't be too sick with me, Emma. I really think it's for the best. Can you come and stay with me for a holiday before you get fixed up with a job, which I'm sure you'll do before long? You're so much more gifted, and impressive, than I am!

Home in two weeks. Do write soon and let me know that you're not too fed up with my decision. It was a nice dream.

Love,
Lucy.

So that was that, thought Emma unhappily as she sat down on the bed. With all her plans shattered, she tried

23

to re-think the future. In tune with her mood, rain was now spattering the window and a grey mist obscured the landscape so that the morning's sunshine now seemed as much of a dream as her own experiences that morning. As she stood up to walk to the window, the book slid off her lap and a flimsy sheet of notepaper fell out as the book hit the floor. Taking it to the window, she studied the scrawled handwriting. Noticing her own name, she smothered any scruples about reading it.

Dear Lucy,

Your letter arrived this morning, and I'm scribbling this on my note pad in the train, as I'm on my way to a conference in Brussels, to urge you to think again about this riding school project. I feel that Emma has persuaded you against your better judgment. She is a very strong-minded young person, used to getting her own way, and you should not allow her to dominate you. This hare-brained scheme will never work and will merely put responsibilities on your young shoulders which could be onerous.

Far better to sell the business, which I'm sure was what Colonel Ackworth intended. It was all he had to leave you, and he saw it as providing you with a capital sum by way of a thank-you for all the help you gave him at the stables. That, at least, is what his housekeeper told me. I've no reason to doubt it. He was very fond of you.

Do think again, my dear, and ignore the impractical enthusiasm of Emma, who can have no knowledge of what is really involved. The business has never done more than just pay its way, according to Jim Brushford, and was the Colonel's hobby, more than anything else. You could land yourself with all kinds of financial troubles which neither you nor Emma Vurney are equipped to handle.

We'll talk about it again when you come home. Sorry the teaching experience of this term has been disillusioning. Not a fair trial, perhaps. A pity to let the last three years' training go for nothing.

Victoria looms. No time for more.
Philip.

So, thought Emma grimly, it had been Philip Rogart's decision more than Lucy's, as she had suspected. Curbing her feeling of betrayal, she could not blame Lucy. Always good-natured, anxious to please, Lucy was not a fighter. And in her heart Emma knew that it was she who had led and Lucy who had followed through all their years at college. Once away from her influence, Lucy would never be able to stand up to that bossy brother.

But as she stood there, gazing with unseeing eyes across the wet landscape, she decided on one thing. She would not go home with her tail between her legs like a whipped dog to her parents, who would be only too glad of this turn of events. She would get work of some kind down here and establish her independence. Not that she did not love her parents. She came from a happy home, and knew it. But she had to strike out on her own some time. And she refused to be beaten.

4

Broomfield

Jean set the table with extra care that evening. Nick was coming to dinner and she wanted to start the evening favourably, to which end she had prepared fresh grape-fruit, curried prawns and a fresh fruit salad, knowing that this menu would suit his taste. She was arranging the accompaniments to the curry when Emma appeared.

"Can I help?"

"No thanks, dear. Everything's in hand."

"Where's Diana? I've found that magazine for her."

"She's at a birthday party."

"That looks super," said Emma, regarding the tray of small dishes which held orange segments, banana slices, cucumber, coconut and chutney, as Jean placed it in the centre of the dining table.

"I like coolers with my curry, and so does Nick," she said.

"It'll be nice to see him again. I took to him."

Jean smiled and fetched dishes for the fruit salad. She hoped that Nick might come up with some helpful advice for Emma this evening. The girl was losing heart, in spite of the brave face she put on her vain search for a job. She had written countless letters, but without success. In her own field, all physical education posts had been filled, as the autumn terms were well under way, and although Emma, in desperation, was no longer particular about the kind of job she wanted, nothing had turned up. Jean eyed her now with sympathetic eyes. She had discarded her favourite garb of sweater and skirt for a plain slate-blue jersey dress which suited her colouring. Her fair hair, swept casually across her forehead and falling to her shoulders, gleamed silkily in the lamplight, but her vivid blue eyes lacked their usual sparkle and, for the past few days, her natural ebullience had been dimmed. Jean had grown fond of her during the three weeks of her stay. Her directness, her spontaneity, were refreshing, and she had brought life to the cottage, establishing a lively friendship with Diana and a warm and confiding relationship with herself, always eager to give a helping hand, laughter and high spirits seldom absent in spite of her present quandary, which was why Jean hoped that Nick might be able to help. Such courage deserved reward.

They fitted in happily together that evening, the three of them. Nick was always excellent company. Witty, urbane, always to be relied upon to ease any social occasion. For Jean, he was an old friend, part of a happier past. For Emma, he was a rare charmer. Mellowed by the excellent wine Nick had brought with him, they enjoyed some music after their meal before Jean brought up the subject of Emma's predicament. Nick eyed her a little quizzically as he listened, mindful of his sister's appeal to him to keep an eye on Emma but reluctant, as always, to get involved.

"Having been out of the country for so long, I'm out of touch. I really don't think I can help. Unless . . . What sort of job are you after?"

"Anything. I'm not in a position to be choosy."

"Wouldn't it be better to go back to your own home ground where your father and your Uncle Joel have business contacts? What about Uncle Joel's own firm?"

"No. I want to be quite independent. They were all so much against my move here. I can't go back. I want to prove what I can make my own way."

"Hm. Well, I did come across an old acquaintance recently who wants an assistant. She's a writer. Jessica Arlingham. An old lady now. I knew her when we both moved in literary circles years ago. She wants someone who can act as secretary, chauffeur, garden help and general dogsbody, from what I can gather. She's handicapped with arthritis and a heart weakness. Can you drive?"

"Yes. I drove the family car when I could get hold of it."

"Type?"

"Yes. I typed minutes of meetings for my father when he was secretary of our residents' association."

"I think she had in mind someone a little older and more experienced, but I'll see if she's found anyone yet and, if not, fix an appointment for you, if you like. She lives in a house a few miles from Dilford. Far too big for her, but she inherited it from her parents and is attached to it. What do you think?"

"Yes, please. I like the sound of it," said Emma, with the optimism which seldom failed her.

Alone with Nick at the end of the evening, Jean apologised for troubling him.

"Not to worry," he said smiling. "I'd already been nobbled by my sister. It's strange how my family has always had the strange notion that I could solve their problems. I, who am the least domesticated of the lot, and have failed miserably in the management of my own domestic affairs."

"What went wrong, Nick? Is it too painful to talk about?"

"Some time, perhaps. Not now, my dear. She's a likeable young woman, is Emma. Such zest! Such expectations from life!" He shook his head as though in sorrow.

"But enough resilience and grit to overcome any disillusionments, I'm sure. I would have loved to have had that much confidence in life. I was always aware that we lived on a knife edge and that happiness is always at risk. A coward soul."

"A sensitive one. That's a handicap in this world."

"Yes. I'm glad Diana has some of Darrel's toughness."

"Where is she, by the way?"

"At a birthday party. In Dilford. She's staying overnight with her friend."

She put on her coat to walk out to the car with him.

"You still have a liking for sporting models, Nick."

"Time I grew out of it, you mean? You could be right. Middle age begins to put the dampers on. By the way, I didn't think it politic to mention to Emma that Jessica Arlingham is in cahoots with her *bête noire*, Philip Rogart. He's her godchild. She seems rather fond of him. Cropped up when we were chatting over coffee at that barn of a house of hers, and Rogart looked in with a book for her. I fancy the connection might be enough to put Emma off."

"It would. She's as hostile as a spitting cat at the mention of his name."

"Ah, youth! So intense. We'll leave her to find out about that serpent lurking in Jessica's garden. She's not, it seems, in a position to pick and choose since she's determined not to return home, and Jessica's a good sort, if a little eccentric. Not a bad writer, either. Thank you, my dear, for a very pleasant evening. You've created a peaceful little oasis here."

"All passion spent," she said a little sadly.

"A state not to be despised in this wicked old world. Stick to the arts, Jean. Much safer and more rewarding."

She watched the car disappear round the bend in the lane and walked slowly back to the cottage through the moonlit garden. It was a cool night, with a few wispy clouds drifting across the sky, playing hide and seek with the moon. The little garden was filled with the bitter-sweet scent of a few late flowering chrysanthemums, ghostly white in the border. It had warmed her heart to have Nick's company again. Their friendship had always been a fond one, with interests in common, and it had never faded in spite of his absence in France for so many years. Correspondence, though sometimes sparse, had never ceased, and when they had met again, they had picked up their friendship as easily as if there had been no interval. It was deeply rooted and went back a long time, to that summer she and Darrel and Nick and his cousin Antonia had spent in Ireland.

29

And in bed that night she found her thoughts returning to that summer long ago, which she remembered as vividly as if it had been last summer, and she wept a little for all that had been lost, before, at last, she fell asleep.

Emma cycled down the laurel-bordered drive towards the red-brick Victorian house called Broomfield in a mood of cautious confidence, for although nothing in her training fitted her for being a secretary-cum-general-assistant to a writer, she felt that she could meet the requirements that Nick had outlined, and surely anybody whom Nick Barbury recommended would be regarded favourably. Emma, by this time, had established Nick on a pinnacle, being of the opinion that he far surpassed anybody she had ever met in looks, charm, wit and achievement.

Propping her bicycle against one of the stone pillars flanking the porch, she grasped the lion's-head knocker – not, she thought, a welcoming lion. The door was opened by a stout, middle-aged woman with rosy cheeks, straight short hair and a pleasant smile.

"You'll be Miss Vurney. Come along in. I'll take you to Miss Arlingham."

She led Emma through a large, stone-flagged hall to a room at the back of the house. There, behind a desk strewn with papers, sat a thin, white-haired woman with a lined face the colour of old parchment, sharp features and pale blue eyes that looked unexpectedly bright and alert in the old face. She waved Emma to a chair on the other side of the desk and regarded her for some minutes in an unnerving silence. When she spoke, her voice was firm, with no hint of the frailty that her appearance suggested.

"Much, much younger than I had in mind, but let me hear what you can do. Nick Barbury is some relation of yours, I gather. He seemed to think you could be useful. I'm handicapped with arthritis and have a tiresome heart condition, so I need someone to deputise for my hands and legs. You type?"

"Yes."

"And drive?"

30

"Yes."

"Why are you applying for this job, Miss Vurney? You have been training for the past three years for a career in physical education, I believe."

Emma explained the circumstances, conscious of a very keen scrutiny from the other side of the desk.

"I see. You want something to tide you over. Well, we may, after all, suit each other. I need someone to tide me over while I try to finish my last book. My doctor does not give me a great deal of time. Not that I pay much attention to doctors. I should want you to live in because needs, although not onerous, crop up at odd times. Not much of a life for a young girl to be cooped up with an old, handicapped woman, but I shan't make great demands of you. I'm as independent as I can be. Just need somebody available for typing my book and correspondence, drive me on the few occasions when I go out and give a helping hand generally. You'd have a good deal of free time. There are days when I can't work. But consider carefully. I can't think this is an appealing occupation for someone as young as you."

"I have to earn my living and I'd like to try this if you're willing to have me."

It seemed to Emma that Miss Arlingham's expression softened as she looked at her.

"Well, I shan't be harnessing you for long, my dear, and maybe the experience will be good for both of us, you at the beginning of your adult life, while I'm at the end. Let me give you my terms, which you are ingenuous enough not to have asked about, and then you can see the bed-sitting room at the top of the house which will be your own domain. It's large and comfortable."

The terms which Miss Arlingham set out seemed very generous to Emma and she accepted them promptly, agreeing to start the following Monday.

"Then ring that bell, Emma. I can't go on calling you Miss Vurney. Mrs Bartlow will show you your room and then we'll have coffee in the sitting-room before you go."

Mrs Bartlow, the woman who had opened the door to her,

31

led Emma up two flights of stairs to a room which stretched across the whole width of the house. One half was furnished as a bedroom, with a divider which was pulled across to separate it from the other half, which was furnished with a couch, two armchairs, a small bureau, television set, radio and book-case. The large sash windows looked across the garden towards the village and the South Downs beyond.

"It was fitted up for Miss Arlingham's brother when he came back here to live after he retired from his job in Australia. It's been left just as it was."

With the late autumn sunshine enriching the rust-coloured carpet and sunflower-patterned curtains, it looked warm and inviting. And nothing that ensued during the remainder of her time at Broomfield that morning caused Emma any qualms about accepting this post. It offered a challenge which she welcomed.

The shock came at the end of her first week's employment.

December had come in with mild, quiet weather, and she was raking up leaves from the front drive on that Saturday morning, enjoying the exercise after the sedentary occupations of the past week, when a car swept into the drive, scattering gravel and forcing her to jump into the laurels. The driver braked and leaned out of the window.

"Sorry. You all right? Good heavens! What are *you* doing here?"

Emma righted herself and eyed the dark face of Philip Rogart with a withering look which combined amazement, indignation and hostility.

"You were going too fast," she snapped.

"Possibly. I've said I was sorry. No harm done." He drove the car up to the house and walked back to Emma, who had resumed her raking with more vigour than accuracy.

"You're the last person in the world I expected to find here. I thought you were in Northumberland. How come?"

Emma leaned on her rake and said coldly, "I came south expecting to join your sister in business, you may recollect. When I got here, I found that the business had been sold, without reference to me. So I was forced to find other work."

"But Lucy wrote to you before you were due."

"I came a little earlier than planned, to find lodgings and inspect the riding school."

"Lucy knew nothing of your early arrival. Didn't you get her letter explaining things?"

"It arrived at my home after I'd left, and was forwarded to me."

"She'll be very upset to hear about this. She only arrived home from Switzerland yesterday. Extended her visit to Grandma's as she was enjoying herself so much."

"I'm glad," said Emma icily.

Philip Rogart eyed her thoughtfully. Then he said, "I'll tell her. She shouldn't have left it so late to inform you of her change of mind. I told her to let you know straight away. But she wasn't to know you'd jumped the gun."

"That," said Emma, trying to keep control of the rage which she felt rising like boiling milk, "is a stupid remark. There was no starting point. It was all settled between Lucy and me months ago. It was your influence that scuppered it. I'm well aware that you manage Lucy's life for her. But there's no point in discussing it further. Do you have an appointment with Miss Arlingham? She's very busy this morning and doesn't like to be interrupted when she's working on her book."

"Really? I'll just try," he said coolly.

Emma looked at him standing there, one hand in his pocket, poker-faced, and wondered why he had always, from their very first meeting, aroused such fierce dislike in her. It was not his appearance, for he was tall, lean, and not bad looking, with crisp black hair, dark eyes, long straight nose and firm mouth. Perhaps it was the calm assurance, the deceptively laid-back manner with which he assumed control as of right in all circumstances. Perhaps because he made her feel so impotent against that assurance. That he wielded complete control over Lucy was not to be doubted. He had never approved of their friendship and had destroyed their partnership plans with ease, thus negating all her endeavours to encourage Lucy to stand on her own feet, lead an independent life of her own choosing. And the taste of that defeat was bitter.

Ignoring him, she picked up the rake and began gathering the leaves together again.

"Where are you staying now, then, Emma? Lucy will want to make amends for having inconvenienced you, I'm sure. She still believes you to be at your home in Northumberland."

"This is my address. I work here. Excuse me," she added, sending a shower of leaves and debris over his shoes.

"*Here?* At Aunt Jessica's? I don't believe it."

Emma looked up like a startled rabbit.

"Aunt Jessica? Is Miss Arlingham your aunt?"

"No blood relation but aunt by adoption, you might say. She was a close friend of my mother's, and is my godmother. But what on earth are you here for?"

"As Miss Arlingham's secretary."

"Oh no," he said, half laughing. "Now I've heard every-thing. Aren't you supposed to be a physical education teacher?"

"What I am, or am not, supposed to be, is none of your business. Kindly keep out of my affairs and confine your attentions to your unfortunate sister."

"So it's warfare, is it?" he observed, amused. "It wouldn't have worked, you know, that riding-school venture. Lucy is just not made for that kind of responsibility. I'm sorry we upset your plans, but it's foolish to be so resentful. I've saved you a deal of trouble, if you but knew it."

"How satisfying to go through life knowing not only what is best for you, but what is best for everyone else, too. If you'd be good enough to get out of my way, I can finish clearing the drive."

"Certainly. Since you won't enlighten me, I must find out from Aunt Jessica what's behind this extraordinary misalliance."

Emma watched him go with loathing in her heart. Only once before in her whole life had she met anybody who aroused in her such violent dislike, and he had been five years old with red hair and she had been a year younger, and had been able to hit him. How odd that she should still remember Ben Tamworth, the bane of her childhood. They had fought on every occasion of their meeting, and honours had been about even, she thought with a reminiscent smile. But it was appalling luck to find herself in a job where she would have to meet Philip Rogart. She wondered how close the tie was between him and Miss Arlingham. Perhaps not close at all. Maybe he was just as much a trial to her as to Emma, and it might be Emma's pleasant duty to keep him at bay. Miss Arlingham wouldn't welcome him this morning, that was certain, for Emma had already discovered that her employer's response to interruption when she was working was brusque, to put it mildly.

But it was more than an hour later, when Emma was taking her last wheelbarrow-load of leaves to the compost heap, when he emerged and waved to her as he got into his car, a wave which she affected not to see.

After she had washed and changed from her gardening clothes into a tartan skirt and sweater, for she was due to spend the rest of the weekend with Jean, she knocked at Miss Arlingham's door to announce her departure.

"Thank you, my dear, for staying to clear the drive. Enjoy the weekend with your friend. You've had an arduous week, but when my creative spring is flowing, which isn't as often as I'd like these days, I have to make the most of it."

"I'm sorry you weren't left in peace this morning. Would you have liked me to put your visitor off?"

"Oh no. Not Philip. He's always welcome. He's a busy person himself and it's good of him to spare the time to keep an eye on my decrepit state. I'm glad of his advice in helping me to cope with this arthritis. What a coincidence that you were at college with his sister."

"Yes," said Emma wrily.

"How attractive you look in that kilt, Emma! Is that your family tartan?"

"We're just south of the Border," said Emma, smiling. "Northumbrians. No claim to any particular tartan."

Cycling along the lanes to Jean's cottage, she felt for

the first time a little homesick for the Northumbrian hills, perhaps out of her element here in the south. Her employer's connection with Philip Rogart had thrown a shadow over her prospects, and did nothing to lessen the hurt of being let down by her friend. She was glad she was spending the rest of the weekend with Jean, whose sympathetic presence was always soothing, and there was always the chance that Nick would look in. This thought lifted her spirits. A pale sunshine emerged, lighting up the silvery plumes of wild clematis that festooned the hedges each side of her and polishing ivy leaves to a glassy surface. Hawthorn berries were plentiful that year and wisps of scarlet and yellow foliage still clung to the brambles so that old December's bareness was softened, and the song of a robin fell sweetly on Emma's ears as she cycled along.

5

Birthday Party

"I'm so sorry, Emma. But perhaps it's all turned out for the best because it will be lovely to have you nearby. I knew you'd be disappointed about the riding school but I'm sure Phil was right. You see . . ." Lucy's voice quavered and she looked troubled.

"Forget it," said Emma. "It's pointless to track back. It was a blow and I think we could have made a go of it, but the decision was made against it and there's an end of it."

"You're always so confident. I expect you think I'm a weakling. I think I am."

"Nonsense. I think you've allowed your brother to dominate you too much but please think no more of it. Tell me about this job you've just accepted. From what you said on the phone, I gather it's not the kind of job we were trained for. That makes two of us."

"That's right," said Lucy, evidently glad to change the subject. "I'm going to try a job as receptionist to the physiotherapist who has rooms in the same building as Philip. He and Phil are good friends. He's a very kind man. I think I shall like working for him. Only hope I'll be good enough for the job."

Philip again, thought Emma. Her battle to encourage Lucy to stand on her own feet and live her own life was going badly. She looked at her friend with exasperated affection. Gentle, soft-hearted Lucy, so anxious to please, so modest. With her large brown eyes, sensitive mouth, silky brown hair and pale complexion, she looked too vulnerable for the hurly-burly of a strident world. And certainly lacking any weapons to withstand the autocratic rule of Philip Rogart.

"Well, we've both landed up in the kind of job we never envisaged and our training and diplomas seem to have been wasted, but I must say I'm quite enjoying working for Miss Arlingham."

"What a strange coincidence that you should take a job with my Aunt Jessica! It seems as though fate means us to keep in touch. I'm really pleased about that, but I can't say I'd care to work for her. She scares me a bit. Makes me feel brainless. But in a way I suppose it's not too dull a job for you, though I think you're much too good for it, because you've always been keen on English literature and working for a writer like Aunt J. isn't too way out."

"It's only temporary, anyway, until the book's finished. And I needed a job. Just look at that beautiful toadstool!" exclaimed Emma, moving from the path through the wood to a large red toadstool emerging bravely from the grass beneath a hawthorn tree.

The sun was beginning to sink as they walked on, the old easy footing restored, scuffling the dead leaves that littered the path. Although the trees were bare, there was no lack of colour in the glow of the setting sun which turned the brown fronds of bracken to a deep gold, warmed the crimson and yellow of the sparse leaves still clinging to the brambles, and added a glow to the holly berries among their shining leaves. At a bend in the path, wild clematis tumbled down a hawthorn tree like a miniature silver waterfall, and overall brooded the moist earthy smell of late autumn. They had set out from Broomfield after lunch on a circular walk which led them back to the house as the sun vanished in red streaks and the air chilled. Tea and some of Mrs Bartlow's feather-light scones and home-made bramble jelly loomed happily in Emma's mind.

Jessica Arlingham watched them walking up the drive, laughing and talking. Unusual to see Lucy so animated. That was the effect Emma had on people. Some people were life-enhancers, she thought, and others life-dimmers.

38

Of the latter, Lucy's father had been a prime example, which perhaps accounted for Lucy's insecurity. She smiled as Emma's laughter ran out, reminded of the days when she and her three sisters and brother were young and this house and garden had been full of life and laughter. It had been a hospitable house, so much coming and going, with tennis parties, cricket in the meadow, dancing when the ballroom craze seized them, musical evenings. Another world. All gone. And she was the sole survivor of the family, having lost her brother, the last of them, two years ago, and that, perhaps, had been the worst loss of all.

She sighed, feeling that she had lived too long, and tried to immerse herself in her notes for the next chapter of her book. But the old ghosts kept intruding and in the end she gave it up. She would like to bring the house to life once more. Give a little supper party, perhaps, on her birthday which fell in December. Nothing to celebrate in being seventy-six, but Christmas would be a week away then, and a certain festive spirit would not come amiss.

When Mrs Bartlow brought in a tray of tea, she was jotting down the names of people she might invite. Few friends now, but Emma and Philip might have some suggestions to make up a suitable number. A pity he and Emma didn't hit if off. He had said little, but it was not difficult to discern that Emma Vurney did not rate highly in his estimation. He even seemed to think that her friendship with Lucy was undesirable, which was understandable, perhaps, in view of past history, but mistaken, in her opinion. About ten in all would be right for her little party. Probably the last birthday she would celebrate, if she read aright her doctor's evasive platitudes, although why he should think she could not bear to contemplate death, she did not know. At her age, seldom out of pain, with all those nearest to her already gone, a lone survivor out of step with the times, it was hardly rational to expect her to have a burning desire to linger. But, then, this was no longer a rational world, she concluded as she pushed the tea tray aside and returned to her notes.

Emma had thrown herself into the preparations for the

supper party with enthusiasm, fired by Miss Arlingham's
inclusion, at Emma's suggestion, of Nick in the party. He
had taken a little persuading, but Emma had prevailed. She
had sent out the invitations, for her employer insisted on this
formality, had spent several hours that morning decorating
the whole house with holly and ivy and fir gathered from
the rambling old garden, had helped Mrs Bartlow prepare
a mammoth fresh fruit salad in the kitchen, and now stood
in front of her bedroom mirror hoping her appearance
would meet with Nick's approval. Not over-conscious of
her looks as a rule, this first experience of falling in love
was introducing a new wish to please. She hoped the classic
simplicity of the delphinium blue dress would please Nick's
fastidious eyes. He would not like frills and fussiness, she
was sure. Her fair hair hung smooth as a bell to the nape
of her neck, gleaming in the light of the lamp. The gold
chain, her twenty-first birthday present from her parents,
was shown off to perfection. It was the first time she had
worn it. She didn't really live a gold-chain life, she thought,
but for Nick, only the best was good enough.

As the door-knocker reverberated through the house,
announcing the first arrival, she ran down the stairs in
happy anticipation.

The party spanned a range of ages from the twenties to
the seventies but, in spite of the wide span, the members all
fitted in with an easy harmony which owed much to Nick's
urbane charm and the joviality of a stout, white-haired,
round-faced man who reminded Emma of Mr Pickwick, and
who went by the name of Jimmy. He was a very old family
friend of Miss Arlingham who had only recently returned
from a world cruise, the details of which he recounted with
humorous gusto, eyes twinkling behind his spectacles.

Emma, glancing round the table, was pleased that the
party had jelled so quickly and the house, for once, had
come to life with laughter and a festive spirit. Her deco-
rations had improved the rather gaunt appearance of the
large dining-room with its heavy Victorian furniture. Miss
Arlingham looked unusually animated at the head of the
table, having Jimmy, with whom she was obviously on

very affectionate terms, on one side of her and Philip on the other.

She had not seen Philip in a party mood before, or indeed in anything but a critical mood as far as she was concerned, but he looked relaxed and smiling as he sipped his wine and listened to the strikingly good-looking young woman who had come with him, and whose name was Monica Ringford. She worked in an art gallery owned by her father, and she and Philip were old friends, according to Lucy, who had seemed a little lukewarm in her attitude. But then Lucy was never at ease with the kind of polished sophistication possessed in such marked degree by Monica. Emma found her impressive, with her sleek black hair, pale complexion, neat regular features and beautiful hands, which she was using to great effect just then. Her black and gold dress was a simple sheath on her slender figure, in contrast with the almost barbaric long gold ear-rings which hung against her cheeks. She had a low, husky voice and was, Emma decided, very sexy. She was turning her large dark eyes to her other neighbour now, Philip's physiotherapist friend, Robert, who would not, Emma thought, be easily dazzled, for down-to-earth stolidity was represented there. Middle-aged, Emma thought, totally reliable and stodgy, with a blunt-featured, squarish face, sandy hair, strongly built, and with a kindly air as he nodded in response to the glamorous Monica before he turned to Lucy, silent beside him, concentrating on her smoked salmon. Lucy hated parties, was desperately shy and usually retired into her shell, but she smiled then at something Robert said and it was obvious that he was trying to put her at ease, for which Emma felt grateful to him. He would be a good employer for Lucy, she thought, and was relieved about this, for she felt very protective towards her friend, so vulnerable in many ways, and had worried a little about her chances of being happy in her new work. She would have been far happier helping in their riding school, though, concluded Emma, dwelling on Philip's dark face with disapproval. Although he was quite good-looking in a saturnine fashion, and no doubt attractive to those of the opposite sex who liked a macho type, she found him utterly unlikeable.

Quitting this object of her dislike, her eyes skimmed over Miss Arlingham's friend and solicitor, Mr Saltburn, and his wife, and returned like a homing pigeon to the object of her delight, the fair-haired, elegant figure of Nick Barbury, sitting opposite her and listening with a rather quizzical expression to Mrs Saltburn enthusing about his book on Yeats, whose poetry she said she adored. Nick, by nature given to understatement rather than the reverse, was too good mannered to register anything but polite attention, but Emma could almost feel him wincing at such effusive utterances.

Watching him, she dwelt joyfully on the prospect of Christmas, now looming. Conscious of a slight feeling of homesickness in the last week or two, she was looking forward to going home for the Christmas week, seeing her family, visiting the clan, riding her pony over the hills, walking the dogs in that spacious landscape she loved. But putting the icing on this delectable cake was having Nick there, too, for her Aunt Jenny had invited him to stay with them for Christmas, and all branches of the family would be getting together throughout the holiday. She was going to ask him if she could drive up to Northumberland with him instead of having to travel by train, and was sure he would agree. To this end, she approached him later that evening. Drawing him away from the party was like cutting out a wayward sheep from the flock, for he had proved very elusive, but at last she caught his arm as the deep discussion he had been having with Miss Arlingham appeared to have come to an end and said, "Come into the conservatory, Nick. There's a superb hippeastrum I want to show you."

Nick's eyebrows shot up.

"I'm an ignoramus where horticulture is concerned. That name suggests nothing but a physical handicap to me."

But he followed her into the adjoining conservatory and there, amid a rather tatty collection of ferns and variegated foliage, Emma presented the flame-coloured flower of the hippeastrum with pride.

"I wanted to ask a favour, Nick."

"Hm. You look very radiant tonight, young Emma. That colour matches your eyes and is very becoming."

"Thank you. Would you be a darling and drive me home for Christmas? I know you're going to Aunt Jenny's, and my home's only ten miles short of Benbury and on the same route."

"My dear Emma, I'd have been delighted to drive you to Northumberland if I'd been going, but I'm afraid I shall be in Italy at that time. I'm sorry to disappoint you," he added gently as he saw her face dim with dismay.

"You mean you're not accepting your sister's invitation? Auntie Barbie was so sure."

"Auntie Barbie?"

"I always used to call her that when she came to look after me when I was a child and she was Miss Barbury. Then she married Uncle Joel and became a real Vurney aunt, but more often than not, I think of her as Auntie Barbie. She'll be so disappointed. Can't you possibly change your plans?"

"Afraid not."

"Why Italy? Christmas is a time for home."

"I've been offered access to some papers that relate to the subject of the book I'm working on now. And I'm not very good at family parties, you know. Nor am I enamoured of the wide open spaces and the grand outdoor life so popular with the Northumberland branches of the clan."

"I had so looked forward to your being with us, and so had Auntie Barbie," she added hastily.

"So sorry." He turned as Philip appeared, glass in hand.

"Hope I'm not intruding, but it's nostalgia time. Aunt Jessica has unearthed an old *Camp Song Book*, and we need some voices to join in. Can you help?"

"I used to perform 'Clementine' very creditably at my grandmother's Christmas parties once upon a time," said Nick.

"Splendid! Come on, Emma. You can manage a few choruses, I'm sure."

And willy-nilly, she followed the two men back to the

party, trying to hide her unhappiness. He only ever saw her as a child, she thought. She was so much in love with him. The way he moved, his voice, his slender elegance, his lazy, amused grey eyes. But he was so elusive. She grasped at a shadow. At home, they could have gone on excursions together, been alone in that splendid countryside, when she had counted on getting to know him better, on his getting to know her better, and her disappointment was deep and painful. She was certainly in no mood to sing old songs, but she dutifully accepted one of the little books of words which Miss Arlingham had unearthed from an old box in the loft.

Slipping out to the kitchen in search of a cold, non-alcoholic drink after the bout of singing had left her throat dry, she found Philip there on the same errand.

"There are some bottles of Perrier in the fridge," she said in response to his enquiry.

"Just the answer. For you, too?"

"Yes, please."

"You've made the house look really inviting, Emma. Congratulations. It's always seemed a sombre place to me. Too big for one old lady."

"It's filled with the ghosts of her past. Her three sisters and brother. What with them and the characters of her novel, I think the here-and-now seldom impinges on Miss Arlingham's mind."

"Perhaps the here-and-now affords little comfort in old age. It's good to see her so lively this evening."

He studied his glass thoughtfully for a moment, then looked up at her and added, "You've brought a cheerful element into her life. I've noticed the difference. Thank you for that, Emma. Aunt Jessica's judgment was better than mine."

His wry tone brought a sparkle to her eyes.

"I can hardly believe my ears. The Christmas spirit must be at work."

"Could be. You're happy working here?"

"Yes."

"A bit lonely, perhaps. No young people around."

"It's good to have Lucy near, and I've friends in Deanswood."

"And your uncle?"

Something in his expression caused her to flush as she said quickly, "Nick's not my uncle. No blood relation."

"An attractive personality. And a very good biographer. I've enjoyed all of his books, and was glad of the chance to meet him. Thanks to you again, Emma."

His eyes were mocking her, she felt, not quite sure how to take him, only knowing that she must cover up. She changed the subject.

"Lucy seems happy in her job, too."

"Yes. Proving very useful to Robert. She tells me that your uncle, sorry, Nick is driving you to your home in Northumberland for a big family party at Christmas."

"He won't be able to come, after all," she said lightly. "He has business in Italy and plans to be there over Christmas. The family will be disappointed."

"And you, I'm sure. I expect Aunt Jessica will let you have the car if you want to drive home rather than use public transport."

"I haven't worked it out yet," said Emma, who had no great love of driving.

"Well, Aunt Jessica won't need the car as Jimmy will drive her to the Eastbourne hotel they've booked for Christmas."

"Yes. I'm glad he managed to persuade her. It's sad to be alone at Christmas. Better to have cheerful strangers around you than nobody at all."

And Emma slid past him back to the party, not wishing to meet those needling eyes any longer. He didn't miss much, she thought. He had shown signs of being human, but that made him more formidable, tempting her to lower her guard. He needed to be watched, this antagonist. With which conclusion she found herself a seat on the sofa between Nick and Lucy and joined in the singing of 'John Peel', the presence of Nick at such close quarters driving all thoughts of Philip Rogart away.

6

Christmas

Emma was not the only person to mourn Nick Barbury's departure for Italy.

"I shall miss you, Nick," said Jean, facing him across the little table in the alcove of the restaurant.

On the eve of his departure, he had invited her to dine with him at a special restaurant he knew which was tucked away on the outskirts of a little village at the foot of the South Downs. Nick would always know a little restaurant where the food was of the highest quality, even if he were stranded in the Gobi desert, she thought, as she eyed him affectionately. This centuries-old cottage, with its white-washed walls and oak beams, small leaded light windows, rose-shaded lamps and leaping open fire, was particularly cosy and attractive in mid-winter.

"These past weeks have been like old times. Very pleasing, my dear."

"Except that we're in our forties instead of our twenties."

"Well, perhaps there are a few compensations. The years that bring the philosophic mind, as Wordsworth puts it. The intensity of youth can be very wearing."

"You were never intense, Nick. Enviably cool, with a light touch. That's why I've always enjoyed our friendship. Something happy and durable and untroubled, and how seldom can you say that of anything in this troubled world of ours?"

"Emotions need to be tightly controlled. Reason must

rule. I've always known this. The one occasion when I forgot it only underlined its validity," he concluded with a dry note in his voice as the waiter poured some wine for his approval.

But hearts, thought Jean, cannot always be controlled. Easier, perhaps, for Nick, who was not a passionate man by nature. Intelligent, intellectually gifted, his blood ran cool. Fastidious, elegant, he was a man born out of his time, she thought. Nothing about him was in tune with the violence and crudity and ugliness of the present age. That he was capable of great kindness she had good reason to know, as had several members of the Rainwood clan, but she could never imagine him swept by passion, and had been surprised when he had forsaken his avowedly chosen bachelor state and married. His work, she had thought, meant more to him than any person ever would. And the marriage had failed. She wondered why. Perhaps because of his total absorption in his work. One day, perhaps, he would tell her. But he was his own man. She might never know.

He lifted his glass to her.

"Let's drink to the philosophic mind."

"How long will you be away, Nick?"

"At a guess, two or three months. I'm going on to America in January. Some papers housed at a university that I want to study."

"And the Rainwood clan has failed to net you for Christmas. Emma is very sad."

Nick studied his glass thoughtfully, then said, "She's a nice kid. Honest and forthcoming. Too highly charged for me. She's met someone her own weight in Philip Rogart, I fancy."

"You don't think there's anything more than a cat-and-dog relationship between them, do you?"

"My dear Jean, I'm no judge of the female mind, but whatever there is between them, it isn't indifference By the way, do you think your daughter is too young to enjoy *Come Hither*? As a dutiful godfather, I feel I should open the door of poetry to her, but I'm not sure whether she's ready for it yet."

"She would love it, Nick. She's just beginning to appreciate poetry, with the aid of a very good teacher at her school who has introduced her pupils to Tennyson."

"Splendid! I took a chance on it, reckoning that your genes and Darrel's would have bestowed on Diana the gift of sensibility. The book's in the car. Don't let me forget to give it to you."

He went on to talk of his grandmother's journal, full of quotations from her favourite poets.

"It's a remarkable social history of this century, in its way. She was a wise woman, was Mirabel Rainwood."

"Would you consider publishing that history?"

"No. Grandma only left me the journal on condition that I never published any of it. She considered it private to the family. I often dip into it. Envy the certainties by which she lived."

It was rare for Nick to forsake the light touch which was his trade mark, and as though aware of this lapse, he refilled her glass and changed the subject to the holiday they had shared with friends in Menton many years ago, one of whom he had recently met again, and they indulged in that favourite pastime of 'Do you remember?' with emphasis on the rosier aspects.

Reflecting on the pleasure of the evening in bed that night, Jean wondered if his departure for several months had been brought forward because he had sensed Emma's growing infatuation with him and thought it politic to remove himself. He had intended to go in the spring. Nick was too shrewd not to grasp the situation, and not unfamiliar with it, she thought wrily. But his observations about Emma and Philip Rogart had surprised her. She had seen Emma droop after Nick's rejection of a family Christmas. There was no room in her heart for any other man, that was obvious, and Philip Rogart was no more than a thorn in her side. Emma was so whole-hearted – in loving and disliking, thought Jean, pounding her pillow, knowing that sleep was going to elude her as thoughts of the past awakened by Nick came back to haunt her. Two lines of a poem came into her head.

There are tiny things that make
The remembering spirit ache.

The truth of that was only too well known to her.

"Oh, Lucy, I don't think so," said Emma, taken by surprise.

"But why not? It's the obvious solution. Your village is only twenty minutes or so off our route to Robert's home in Kelso. No trouble at all to make that small diversion. It will save you heaving luggage about on public transport. It's an awkward journey from here, and you don't want to drive yourself all that way in that old car of Aunt Jessie's. I thought you'd jump at it."

Lucy's expression was hurt and puzzled. Robert's invitation to her and Philip to spend Christmas with his family in Kelso had seemed to her a golden opportunity to solve Emma's travelling problems.

"Do you want to spend Christmas with Robert Bedfield's family? I mean, they're nothing to you. You usually dislike meeting strangers, let alone staying with them for several days," said Emma.

"Phil knows them. Robert's a very old friend of Phil's."

"But not yours. You're not automatically part of Phil's baggage. I thought you were all set up for Christmas at home."

"We were, until Robert's invitation came. And I've known him, through Phil, ever since I was in socks. On and off. I'm looking forward to going."

"I didn't realise he was more than a friendly employer," said Emma slowly.

"Do say you'll make a fourth in the car. We're taking ours. I'd like your company on the journey. And it would make things much easier for you."

Emma hesitated. It was hard to explain to Lucy her reluctance to accept any favours from Philip and her dismay at the thought of a day shut up in a car in his company. But Lucy's brown eyes were pleading, and it was hard to find any rational objection to a proposition which would save her an arduous journey north.

49

"Well, thank you. It's very kind of Robert."

And thus Emma found herself waiting in the hall of Broomfield, suitcase beside her and a separate hold-all containing Christmas presents at her feet, on a cold grey morning with none of the magic of Christmas Eve about it, in Emma's opinion, the disappointment of Nick's withdrawal still clinging to her like the wispy fog that shrouded the trees in the garden and quite obscured the downs.

The grey Citroën drew up punctually with Philip driving and Robert beside him. Emma joined Lucy in the back and greeted them with as good an act of Christmas cheer as she could muster.

Instead of clearing as the day wore on, the fog tended to thicken, although patchy, and they opted for a quick snack lunch at a restaurant off the motorway as they wanted to arrive at their destination before darkness added to the difficulties posed by the fog. Emma was glad when they left the monotony of the motorway for the quieter roads of Northumberland but by then it was nearly dark, fog having slowed them down, and driving was becoming hazardous and difficult. Lucy went silent, her face tight and pale. Philip nosed the car along cautiously while Robert studied the map. Through the rolling fog, Emma thought she recognised a landmark. Robert was uncertain where they were. Unearthing a torch, she slipped out of the car to study a signpost at the junction of three lanes. She recognised the names.

"Straight on takes you to crossroads. Turn right there and our house is about half a mile further on. There's a ditch each side of the road. Will it help if I go ahead with the torch?"

"Highly risky," said Philip. "We might send you into the ditch. We'll manage."

"You must stay the night with us. You can't go on in this," said Emma.

Philip braked as a rear light pricked through the swirling fog. They passed the wraith-like form of a cyclist and came to the crossroads. Lucy, tense and silent, was hunched up in the corner of the car. Emma, peering out of the window, caught a glimpse of the landmark she was looking for.

"There's the farm. About fifty yards on, Philip. I'll get out then and find the drive. They'll have the gates open."

"Right."

Torch held aloft, Emma took up her position.

"I'm on the left side, Philip. It's a wide drive, you can give me about a yard. I don't fancy the ditch – it's usually full of stinging nettles and mud," she called cheerfully, anxious to relax Lucy.

"Do my best," said Philip.

The front door was open, the light streaming out, revealing her parents and two barking retrievers who leapt at Emma. Engulfed in her mother's arms with the dogs pawing at her back, it was some moments before Emma could get her breath back and introduce her party. Lucy was known from previous holidays she had spent with Emma but, overwhelmed with relief at their safe arrival, her parents welcomed them all as though part of the family, and refused to admit any possibility of their travelling on that night.

"Even if the fog lifts, you must be far too tired to drive any further tonight," declared Emma's mother, noting Philip's reddened eyes and Lucy's chalk-white cheeks. "We've plenty of room. Robert, you'd better phone your parents straight away. They will be worried. What weather for Christmas Eve!"

And Joyce Vurney took charge with a cheerful decisiveness which reminded Philip of Emma and set him wondering who won when the sparks flew between mother and daughter, as they surely sometimes must with two such positive characters.

Refreshed by tea and hot baths, the three men and Lucy gathered round the log fire in the sitting-room while Emma helped her mother prepare supper.

"We're all starving. Only had a snack lunch on the way. Good thing you've got lots of food in, Mum," said Emma, depositing a joint of ham on the dining table and surveying a bowl of salad, basket of hot rolls, a Stilton cheese, dishes

51

of fruit and nuts and a large pile of mince pies keeping warm
on an adjoining hot tray.

"Thought I'd better be prepared for the weather stepping in and spoiling our plans."

"And what was finally arranged after all the 'Come to
us – no, come to us' pother?"

"Weather permitting, we are spending tomorrow with
Aunt Jenny and Uncle Joel, who have a big party planned."

"The Castleton lot, too?"

"Giles and Kit and the boys, yes," said her mother rather
coolly.

"And Boxing Day?"

"At Castleton. All of us."

"Two days with those Coalville twins!"

"What about some seasonal good will, dear? There will be
a big party. And you get on well enough with Simon."

"I'd sooner we were having a family party at home. I
prefer to meet them on my own ground."

"You were keen enough on the idea when we talked
about it on the phone the other week."

But that, thought Emma, was when she thought Nick
would be part of the family gatherings.

"Oh well, perhaps it'll be too foggy to travel," she said
cheerfully as she distributed wine glasses.

"They're very agreeable young men, Robert and Philip.
I got quite the wrong impression from your remarks about
Lucy's brother. I expected some overbearing, loud-mouthed
boor. He's quite charming."

"He can put on a smooth act. The season of good will
prevents me from saying more," concluded Emma, her eyes
teasing her mother.

"Tell them we're ready, and see that the dogs are kept in
the sitting-room. You know how your father dislikes them
in here, cadging food."

"Sure," said Emma blithely. It was good to be home.

The laws of hospitality demanding that animosities be put
aside, Emma found the evening passing most pleasurably, a
little to her surprise. Recovered from the fatigue and strain
of their journey, the travellers did full justice to the meal

and, helped by the wine, a festive spirit prevailed. Robert and her father discovered a mutual interest in climbing which resulted in an invitation to Robert to come and sample the Cheviots in the spring, Lucy was unusually lively and at ease, and her mother seemed to have fallen unreservedly for the dark charms of Philip, both being absorbed in talk of books by the time coffee came round. That much of the harmony was due to her parents, Emma was well aware. Theirs had always been an open house and her parents welcomed friends and strangers alike with unfussy hospitality.

Afterwards, they sat round the log fire listening to a carol service, Emma and Lucy joining in with the more familiar carols, Lucy's voice thin, clear and true, Emma's more robust.

The cloud which had sat heavily on Emma since Nick's withdrawal began to lift that evening and, singing 'The First Noël' as she sat on the hearthrug and roasted chestnuts for the party, she felt happy and ready for Christmas. Lobbing a hot chestnut to Philip, who hastily tossed it from hand to hand, she was rewarded with an odd, rueful little smile and a nod that had a hint of the conspiratorial about it. A conspiracy of what? Strategic warfare? Wary conciliation? It couldn't be a kind of affection, could it? Impossible. A trick of the firelight. Her eyes shifted from his gaze, which was thoughtful now, to Floss, the golden retriever whose weight was across her feet. Pushed aside, Floss straightaway rolled over on her back, limp paws at rest, for Emma to rub her. Candy, Floss's daughter, lying at her master's feet, lifted a lazy head to observe these proceedings, then flopped back again with a single thump of her tail.

Emma threw another log on the fire and settled for singing 'Oh Come, All Ye Faithful'.

Christmas morning dawned grey and damp but clear of fog. In the half-light, Emma collected the dogs for a quick walk through the neighbouring wood before breakfast and ran into Philip, who had been checking the car, which was parked at the side of the house. A knocking in the engine had been bothering him towards the end of their journey.

"Good morning, Philip. Happy Christmas."

He straightened up, fielded Candy, who had hurled herself at him ecstatically as though welcoming him after a long absence, and stroked her silky head as he said, "And a very happy Christmas to you, Emma. How fresh and blooming you look, so early in the morning."

"Are you a slow starter then, like my father? He's a zombie until he's had his breakfast coffee."

"I come to at a measured pace, shall we say?"

"Is the car O.K.?"

"Yes, as far as I can see. May I join the exercise party?"

The path through the wood was covered with the decaying leaves of autumn through which the dogs scampered, disappearing at frequent intervals, noses to the ground, as they picked up intriguing scents. A pale, rosy light slanted through the trees as the rising sun broke through the clouds and warmed the muted colours of the winter woodland. The magpie pattern of the birch trunks stood out against the dark tracery of elms, the green of holly and the red flush of dogwood. The only sound to break the silence was the chattering of a blackbird disturbed by the dogs.

Emma, savouring the damp, earthy smell, stepped out briskly, happy to be back in her own countryside, at ease, for once, in Philip Rogart's company.

"It was kind of your family to give us such a warm welcome, Emma. A happy interval for us, and an unexpected Christmas bonus."

"Our pleasure," she said lightly.

"Lucy has often told me how beautiful your home country was, but even her enthusiasm didn't do it justice. A lovely environment to grow up in."

"Yes. I love the Border country. Walking, riding, it's unbeatable."

"Do you have stables handy?"

"No. But I've a pony that my Uncle Joel looks after for me. My aunt and my cousin ride a bit and keep her exercised while I'm away. They live only a few miles away and the arrangement works very well. We're due there for the Christmas family party today. Then to another branch of the family at Castleton on Boxing Day, so there won't be much chance for riding, I'm afraid.

"Yours is a large clan, I gather."

"Not the Vurneys. But through Uncle Joel marrying into the Rainwood clan, we got sucked in, as it were. At least, into the Northumberland branches of Rainwoods. The other branches stretch like an octopus across Surrey and Sussex, according to Nick, who stands warily on the fringe."

"Not a family man."

"He was very fond of his grandmother, the matriarch of the family, who died in the autumn. I met her once when I was only four years old but I've never quite forgotten her."

"Well, she had a very gifted grandson in Nick. Not that he throws his weight about. On the contrary. Stands aside and views the rest of the world with detached amusement, I feel. But not an easy man to know. His defences are too good."

This Emma knew only too well, but was not inclined to admit it. She only knew that she was in love with Nick and had faith that time would bring deeper understanding.

"An attractive chap," went on Philip, as Emma remained silent. "He must be very wily to have escaped capture and remained a bachelor."

"He did marry. Divorced," said Emma curtly, not liking his sceptical tone.

"Ah. Detachment like his isn't all that comfortable to live with. Nor the wholesale absorption in writing that shuts out the rest of the world."

"You make him sound a very cold fish. I can assure you that he's not. And why you should think that one encounter at a party enables you to sit in judgment, I don't know."

"I was only generalising about writers. Their work inevitably detaches them from the here and now for long periods of time. No need to be so touchy."

"It sounded personal to me."

"Nothing adverse, then. I was merely observing that people whose emotions rule their minds can find detachment in the person they care for very hard to live with. I know nothing about Nick Barbury's personal affairs. His wife may have been an impossible woman. We all make mistakes."

"I know nothing about it," said Emma stiffly, the spirit of good will between them evaporating rapidly. She was in no doubt that he regarded her as one of those females whose emotions ruled their minds.

"Nick Barbury is obviously a prickly subject for you. I'll say no more."

The circular walk had brought them in sight of the house again. The baying of one of the dogs broke the silence. Candy had treed a squirrel and was leaping at the trunk in a frenzy of barking, joined by Floss a moment later. Emma ran through the trees and collected them, glad of the distraction, annoyed with herself for losing her cool yet again with Philip Rogart, to her own disadvantage.

"Squirrels always drive them mad," she observed as he joined her. "I'm for breakfast. I'm starving."

And, stepping out, they completed their walk in silence.

The Kelso party left immediately after breakfast, having made arrangements to pick Emma up on the return journey. Standing in the porch with her parents, waving them off, Emma was not sorry to see Philip go. She always found him a disturbing force, throwing stones into the smooth surface of her pond, leaving ever-widening circles. Now he had re-awakened the ache of disappointment at Nick's absence.

Alone in her bedroom, she took from her shoulder bag a small folded photograph holder. In this she had inserted a photograph of Nick that she had cut from the wrapper of his latest biography. His classically handsome face looked out at her with a cool, faintly ironical expression as though disclaiming the fulsome praise of his literary achievements printed in the blurb below. If one judged from that photograph, Philip's observations might be deemed accurate. But it was all she had, and her heart was warm with love as

56

she looked at that face, tantalising, holding out a promise of such pleasure to mind and heart and body, uniquely charming and as elusive as a shadow. She longed for closer intimacy, for the light-hearted friendship he offered to grow into something deeper. It would, she thought. It must.

7

Lucy

March had come in with sunny, breezy days and the sunken lane which climbed up to the downs was bright with the heralds of spring. The hawthorn in the hedgerow was starred with green, catkins swung from hazel trees as the breeze caught them and celandines gleamed with buttery gold on the grassy banks. Emma and Lucy had reached the top of the climb and came out on to the smooth turf of the downs before Lucy dropped her bombshell.

"I've some news for you, Emma. I'm engaged to be married. To Robert."

Emma turned a startled face to her. "You're joking!"

"Of course I'm not."

"Robert Bedfield? But he's years older than you, Lucy. Middle-aged."

"Thirty-four isn't middle-aged."

"But . . . but . . . he's middle-aged in his ways. You can't want to tie yourself down before you've had a chance to enjoy your freedom. You're only just out of college, for heaven's sake."

Lucy looked distressed. "I've known Robert for years. He's a dear person. I . . ." She broke off and looked away.

"Lucy, is this Philip trying to organise your life again?"

"Of course not. Why should he?"

Emma could think of several reasons and, although she regretted her too-hasty tongue afterwards, gave voice to them now. "To suit his own plans, perhaps. He may have in mind joining up with the glamorous Monica and not want to leave you alone. He may want to be rid of the house and return to his flat. But you've your own life to live, Lucy. Don't go into this just because it seems a soft option. Robert's a nice enough person, I'm sure, but too old and staid. A friend, yes. But have you really thought it through? You haven't seen anything of life yet. We could travel the world, you and I, once we've got a little cash behind us. Don't put yourself in a cage."

"You don't understand, Emma. I'm not adventurous, like you."

"Well, don't be upset. I'm sorry if I've hurt you, but I'm truly only concerned for your happiness. Just promise me that you'll give it more thought. Perhaps ask Robert to wait a bit before you finally commit yourself. That can't do any harm."

"I'll think about it," said Lucy. "Let's not talk about it any more. What's been happening on your front? It's a long time since I've seen you. Not since Christmas. My fault, I know."

With Lucy's absence now explained by the intrusion of Robert Bedfield into her life, Emma masked her dismay and turned to other matters, for Lucy looked very unhappy and would need time to ponder Emma's words. That she was not too certain herself about this unsuitable engagement was obvious. She was so pliable. No doubt Philip had connived at this.

"My news? Well, Miss Arlingham's book is three-quarters finished and she's anxious to press on with it, but she's not been too well lately. I'm a little worried about her. And we've a visitor staying with us, some very distant relative of hers, who's upsetting the working routine a bit. Have you ever heard of Maurice Braidon?"

"No. But then I've never had a lot to do with Aunt Jessica. I've always found her a bit forbidding. Where does he come from, this visitor?"

"South Africa. A freelance journalist. Says he's thinking of returning to England. He's the son of a cousin of the man Miss Arlingham's oldest sister married, so it's a very remote connection and Miss Arlingham has never known of his existence. I don't much care for him, though he's genial enough. Hasn't Philip mentioned his arrival to you?"

"No. But Phil's been very busy lately. He's been in Brussels this week on a visit to some European conference of osteopaths. How long is this visitor staying?"

"Very vague about moving on. I'm wondering if he has ideas about being next of kin and benefiting from Miss Arlingham's will. He's very kind and courteous to her, flattering her work, which he has studied thoroughly. I don't think she's likely to be taken in by him, and I may be misjudging him, but the atmosphere isn't as it was before he came."

"I'll mention it to Phil when he gets back. He's very fond of Aunt Jessica. Wouldn't want her to be imposed on or troubled."

A lark got up ahead of them and they stopped to watch its spiralling flight until it hovered high above them, pouring out its liquid melody. The happiest of all birdsong, thought Emma, as they continued along the chalky footpath, the smooth contours of the downs all around them and a small, shining triangle of sea visible through a gap in the distance. Responding to the mood of spring, with the sun warm on her face and the breeze stirring her hair, Emma dismissed the shadows cast by Lucy's news and the newcomer into her working life at Broomfield, to enjoy the sense of physical well-being and the joys of the countryside in the springtime of the year. Nick would be back in two weeks' time. And that thought made the landscape even brighter.

But by the time they dropped down to the village of Deanswood, where they planned to lunch, Emma could not but be aware that Lucy, in spite of responding amiably to Emma's chatter on the way, had not shared her happy mood. She looked pale and withdrawn and hardly glanced at the menu in the café, opting for a cheese salad, half of which she left.

"Do you feel all right, Lucy?" asked Emma anxiously.

"Of course. Just a bit tired. Had a late night. Went with Robert to the Benson theatre in Dilford to see *The Mikado.*

Very jolly. I've had those jingly tunes in my head ever since."

Emma hesitated about bringing up the subject of Lucy's engagement to Robert again, and as though sensing the possibility, Lucy hastily changed the subject by talking about a prospective holiday in Switzerland with her grandmother. She refused Emma's invitation to come back to Broomfield for the afternoon and hear some records of ballet music which Emma had recently bought, pleading some urgent shopping in Dilford. Knowing Lucy's love of ballet and dislike of shopping, Emma drew her own conclusions about the validity of this excuse, and felt a little worried as she saw her off on her bus and made her own way back to Broomfield. Lucy was so sensitive. Had she said too much? Been too forthright in her opposition to her engagement? But Lucy needed protection. Philip might well be shepherding her into a match which could at best only be tolerable and very likely result in unhappiness and frustration for her. Perhaps, though, she should have presented her views more gently. Not for the first time, her impetuous tongue had run away with her. She had wounded Lucy, and that was the last thing in the world she wished to do. And the thought that Lucy needed saving from herself did not altogether reassure her as she walked up the Broomfield drive.

Miss Arlingham had given her the day off as she was resting after a bad night and, faced with the presence of Maurice Braidon about the place, Emma decided to call in at Jean's cottage that afternoon. She had an open invitation there at any time and Emma had grown very fond of the quiet, sympathetic woman who had welcomed her so kindly from the first days of her arrival in Sussex, and whose loneliness Emma sensed. And from Jean she might have more news of Nick.

The uneasiness which Emma felt about Lucy that weekend was justified in devastating manner on the following Monday evening. Philip had arrived to see Miss Arlingham and, spotting his car as it drew up, Emma had escaped to her room, not wishing to meet him. She was writing a letter home when some time later there was a knock on her door and Philip came in, looking as genial as an east wind.

"Hullo. Did you have a useful trip to Brussels?" she asked, not caring for his expression.

"Yes, thanks. I want to talk to you, Emma."

"Oh, yes. Have a seat," she said, waving to the armchair, remaining poised at the little bureau, biro in hand, as though not intending to be diverted from her letter for long.

He ignored this invitation and went across to the window, staring out for a few moments before turning to face her. "I don't know whether you're aware of it, but you've caused Lucy great distress. You've destroyed all her happiness and confidence in her engagement to Robert by your bossy notion that you always know best what's good for other people."

Emma's lips tightened at his cold, controlled tone. "When I see a friend heading for disaster, I feel a duty to try to head it off."

"And you're an infallible judge of what is disaster in such personal matters, are you?"

"If Lucy's confidence is shattered by what I advised, she can't be sure herself. And it's too important a matter to be unsure about."

"You know how impressionable Lucy is, and that she sets great store by what you say. Why, heaven knows. You've little experience in life, you're self-willed and cocky, you know it all: what's best for you, what's best for Lucy. You're the last person in the world Lucy should listen to."

If he had spoken in rage, it would not have struck so hard, but his words were cold, measured and spoken with conviction, and she felt pierced by his daggers. Then temper came to her aid.

"If you've finished, will you please leave my room? You've always disliked me, thought me a bad influence for Lucy. Probably because I threaten your management of her life, which would put her in the chains of a loveless marriage to suit your convenience, perhaps."

"So it was your words that suggested that I wanted to be rid of her, as well as everything else you could throw up against Robert. You've done untold damage, and you just haven't a clue, have you?"

"What do you mean? I care for Lucy's happiness."

"Rubbish! Let me try to make you understand. Perhaps I should have enlightened you before, but Lucy doesn't like to remember it. You know our parents were killed in an accident when Lucy was fifteen. You probably don't know that our father was a sadist and a bully, and Lucy was an easy target. He reduced her to a frightened child on the verge of a mental breakdown. I'd left home before she reached that stage and didn't realise how bad the situation was. Lucy never said much. She was in the car when my parents were killed. She escaped unhurt, but the shock on top of everything that child had suffered proved the last straw, and she was in a hospital for mental illness for a spell. She recovered, but she's vulnerable. She'll never be tough like you, Emma. She needs a sheltered life to give her confidence. Robert will give her that. She was happy at the idea until you put your spanner in the works," he concluded bitterly.

"I didn't know."

"But you must have known that Lucy was vulnerable, lacking all self-confidence. That's why she's so drawn to you. You're nothing if not positive and self-confident," he said drily.

"But Robert is middle-aged. Staid. There's an enormous gap in their ages."

"Nothing like as great as the gap between you and Nick Barbury. Has that occurred to you?"

Flushing scarlet, Emma was speechless at this knock-out. Philip observed her with cold satisfaction. In the silence that fell between them, she burned with humiliation and dismay. It was he who broke the silence.

"Robert has known Lucy ever since she was a schoolgirl. He knows her history. He cares for her and will give her security and a sense of belonging, which she's never had. As well as threatening that, you've put it into her head that she's been a burden to me. That she ought not to tie me down. Between that and the doubts you've sown about Robert, she's in the kind of mental distress and instability that we hoped was a thing of the past."

"I couldn't have known. I'm sorry. I only spoke honestly, as I felt. Is there anything I can do?"

"I'd have said keep away from Lucy, but I know she's attached to you. Perhaps now you know how vulnerable she is, you'll tread more carefully. I leave it to you to repair the damage if you can, but when you sow doubts, they're not easily dispelled. I think I've managed to erase your picture of me as the scheming brother anxious to be rid of her. I'm very fond of Lucy. She had the sort of childhood no child should have."

"Why should your father have been so cruel to Lucy? Such a gentle person, who would never defy him?"

"He did it as a way of getting back at my mother. It was a very unhappy marriage. Our home life was appalling. I was able to escape. Lucy wasn't. I've hopes that Robert will make up for it, if you haven't sabotaged things."

He left then, as though unable to waste more words on her. Emma, shattered, put her head in her hands. She had only two thoughts clear in her mind amidst the chaos he had caused: she must try to put matters right for Lucy, and she would never forgive or forget Philip Rogart's assessment of her for she had only spoken, mistakenly or not, out of a deep affection for his sister.

8

The Intruder

Driving back from the village a few days later, Emma was not best pleased to see Maurice Braidon doing some repairs to the front gates. She had been despatched to collect the pills Miss Arlingham needed for her angina. She lifted a hand in salute as she drove up to the house, wondering how long he proposed staying with them. He followed her up the drive.

"Lovely day," he observed. "How about a stroll before lunch?"

"I've a pile of typing waiting for me."

"Too good a day to spend indoors."

"I'm a working girl," she said lightly and made for the door, but he waylaid her, a hand on her arm.

"Just ten minutes, then, Emma. Something I want to discuss with you."

They walked across the lawn towards the far boundary, a hedge which divided them from a field in which a group of donkeys and a couple of horses grazed.

"That some kind of a home for old age pensioners?"

"Yes. A sanctuary for donkeys and horses rescued from ill treatment."

"Hm. Who owns it? Is it part of your land rented out, or what?"

"Not ours. I don't know whether Jill Sandgate owns it or rents it."

"You know her?"

"I give her a hand now and again when I've some free time."

65

He looked thoughtful for a moment, then said, "The old lady looked very poorly this morning, I thought."

"Yes. She should rest more, but she's anxious to get this book finished."

"What does the doctor say?"

"She doesn't see him very often. Her heart is tired. There's not much he can do about that."

"I suppose not. After all, she's seventy-six. A good age. Shame she's so alone. No family left, except me."

"Will you be returning to South Africa soon?"

"No definite plans. Don't like to leave the old lady, to tell you the truth. Needs a man about the place, if you ask me."

"She's very independent and capable," added Emma firmly.

"And you're a great help to her, my dear. But she could be a prey to hangers-on with an eye to the main chance, you know. This chap Rogart, for example. He's no relation. Why does he hang around?"

"His mother was Miss Arlingham's closest friend. Philip is her godchild and has known her all his life. And has been of great help to her in coping with her arthritis."

"He's some sort of bone-setter, isn't he?"

"An osteopath. Is that all? I must be getting back."

"What's the hurry? A pretty girl like you, shut up with an invalid? Not much of a life for you. How about an evening at a disco in Dilford? Not exactly an exciting town but I believe they have a disco at the Grange Hotel on Saturday nights."

Emma looked pointedly at the hand which he slid round her waist, then looked up at his smiling face. He was dark, with a tanned complexion, small eyes, a sensual mouth and very white, even teeth. Not bad looking, she thought, and exceedingly objectionable.

"Not my scene. I can't stand the noise," she said briefly and, disengaging herself, turned for the house.

"Well, we'll fix a quiet little dinner some time, then. Those blue eyes of yours quite throw me, Emma."

She was spared the necessity to reply by the arrival of Joe Bartlow pushing a barrow full of grass cuttings.

"The lawns look lovely after their first cutting, Joe," said Emma.

"Aye. Always like the smell of new-mown grass. Just the thought of all the cutting to come that's a bit sobering."

"I'll give you a hand. I quite like being behind a mower."

He smiled his thanks, his kindly, wrinkled face the colour of a russet apple, and carried on round the house towards the compost heap.

"Getting a bit past it, isn't he?" observed Maurice.

"Not a bit of it. He manages this large garden splendidly."

"With your help, I bet. You work hard here, Emma. I can see that. You must let me take you out in the evenings, give you a break. You deserve some fun."

Men, thought Emma. Chauvinist men, who thought their company must spell fun, that any female would think it a privilege to be taken out by them as a reward and compensation for their dreary lives. Suffering just then from extreme hostility to the male ego, fanned to a blaze by the incursions of Philip Rogart into her life, she was in no mood to pander to this oily man with his inquisitive tongue.

"I choose my own kind of fun, thank you, and I don't think it bears much relation to yours. Excuse me."

She ran on, his laugh following her.

Busily typing from Miss Arlingham's difficult manuscript that afternoon, she thought she heard a call from the adjoining study and found her employer hunched over her desk, her face screwed up with pain.

"My pills, Emma. I left them in my bedroom." She seemed to have difficulty in breathing, and Emma flew up the stairs.

Miss Arlingham slipped the pill under her tongue and, noticing Emma's distressed face, said jerkily, "Nothing to worry about. I usually take a pill in good time. Keep them with me. Careless to leave them elsewhere. Give me a minute or two."

"Can I fetch you anything? Brandy?"

"Nothing, dear. It's easing now. Nothing to worry about. I'm used to these attacks. Perhaps a pot of tea would be a good idea."

When Emma came back with the tea, Miss Arlingham seemed her normal self again and surveyed Emma with an affectionate little smile.

"Don't look so concerned, dear. You haven't seemed your usual bright self lately. Am I working you too hard?"

"Oh no."

"Is anything troubling you here?"

And Emma, who had no intention of burdening Miss Arlingham with her troubles, anxious only to reassure her, smiled and said, "I love my work here. I just wish I could persuade you to rest more. You look so tired."

But if Miss Arlingham looked physically frail, her mind was as keen as ever.

"Is Maurice bothering you?" she asked, her eyes searching.

"No. I think we were cosier without him, though," she added cautiously.

"Yes. I doubt he'll stay much longer. He's not important. Just let me know if he bothers you."

"Not to worry," said Emma cheerfully. "I can handle him, as long as I know that offending him won't upset you."

"One of the few advantages of being as old as I am, dear Emma, is knowing what's important and what is not worth bothering about. Maurice is not important to me. He's played no part in my life and is a stranger. I'm prepared to let him nose around here if he doesn't overstep the mark because I can't be bothered to do otherwise. He'll probably be moving on as soon as he's sized us up," she concluded with an ironical little smile.

Emma, reassured by this evidence that Miss Arlingham was not being duped by her distant relative, poured her another cup of tea, only to be disconcerted by the next question.

"And what's the trouble between you and Philip? On

the few occasions when you meet here, you're both so frigidly polite to each other that the temperature drops immediately from spring to mid-winter."

"Well, we've never exactly seen eye-to-eye," said Emma, thinking that this was the understatement of the century.

"Mm. Too much alike, perhaps. Well, at least it's better than boredom. Nothing like a rush of hostility to warm the blood. I wish I could still feel strongly about anything or anybody, but I can't any longer."

"You'll feel stronger now that the summer's in front of us," said Emma gently, her heart wrenched with pity for this gallant old lady who battled with the pain of crippling arthritis and angina with so little complaint and an indomitable spirit.

"We'll finish the book, anyway, my dear. I think I'll leave it for today, though. Jimmy's joining us for dinner this evening. He's just returned from a holiday in the Caribbean, so we shall be regaled with his adventures."

"He's a dear."

"Yes. I expect it's hard for you to imagine that he was quite the handsomest young man of the many who came to our parties here, and an ace tennis player. We all fell in love with him at different times. So long ago," said Miss Arlingham, looking out of the window at the old tennis court, "and yet it's as vivid to me as though it was only yesterday, that age of innocence."

Emma removed the tea tray and left her to her memories, trying to visualise the tubby, genial Jimmy as a handsome young man leaping about the tennis court, serving and volleying his opponents to defeat, the idol of the four Arlingham girls.

9

Man Trouble

In the café opposite to the church in Dilford High Street, Emma placed on the floor at her feet the parcel of books she had fetched from the bookshop for Miss Arlingham and waited for Lucy, working out what to say to repair the damage she had unwittingly caused. She came in ten minutes later, a plastic carrier bag in each hand, apologising.

"Sorry, Emma. Got held up in the cleaner's."

With her bags stowed on a spare chair, Lucy sat opposite Emma with a faintly uneasy air about her. She looked pale, with shadows under her eyes. They ordered coffee and Emma wasted no time.

"Lucy, I want to say I'm sorry for leading forth about your engagement to Robert last weekend. I spoke without any knowledge of him. Silly of me. I suppose it was because it was such a surprise. I didn't stop to think. You know me. I so often jump in regardless. Just forget it. I meant well. The road to hell is paved with good intentions, and all that."

Lucy's face broke into a smile.

"You mean you've had second thoughts?"

"Yes. I think I was talking through my hat. I know next to nothing about your Robert. If you feel sure about being happy with him, then that's all that matters and I'm happy, too."

"When you know him better, Emma, I'm sure you'll agree that I'm lucky. I do so want you two to be good friends. I've had an awful week, worrying about it, but

70

last night I talked it over with Robert again, and I've promised to let him know tonight whether I want to back out. I'm meeting him for dinner in Deanswood. It won't make any difference to our friendship, he says. But now you feel differently about it, it makes me feel more sure, too."

"But it doesn't matter what I think, Lucy. It's what you feel that matters," said Emma, finding her friend's lack of confidence difficult to comprehend, in spite of Philip's revelations. She could not imagine being influenced by any outsider in similar circumstances.

"It's such a big step, and I'm not just thinking of myself. I think Robert may find me very disappointing. I'm such an inadequate sort of person."

"If you're going to indulge in one of your self-denigratory moods, Lucy, I shall lose patience. If you can't trust your own judgment, you can surely trust Robert's. He knows what he's doing. And if you do agree to marry him, he'll be a very lucky man. You're too sweet-natured for this world, you know. And this coffee's half-cold. Is yours?"

"Not too bad."

"Which means it is," said Emma, and told the waitress so. Not too pleased, she took their cups away and returned some minutes later, banging them down on the table with a vigour that threatened the contents.

"Shan't come here again," observed Emma. "At the price they charge, it should at least be hot. I can't discern any flavour, either, although it's such a fierce colour. It dazzles to deceive."

Lucy laughed, looking happy and relaxed, to Emma's relief.

"You always do me good, Emma," she said.

"Not always. Not last Saturday."

"You were right to speak your mind. I sprung it on you. Now you've had time to think more about it, I'm so glad that you see it my way."

"And that is?"

"Why, to marry Robert. Make a happy, secure home. He's so kind and understanding. I think we can make the sort of home I never had. That's my hope, anyway."

71

And Emma was silenced, forced to go along with an engagement which in her heart she still viewed with misgiving, but realising that Lucy's needs were very different from her own. All she ventured now was, in a casual tone, "I suppose you won't be in a tearing hurry. A lot to plan. Finding a home and all that."

"Robert doesn't want to wait. Once I've made up my mind he sees no point in delay, because a friend of his has just been moved from the bank where he works to a branch in the Midlands and he wants to sell his cottage. Halfway between here and Deanswood. It's quite small but has half an acre of garden and Robert thinks we'd be comfortable there, and convenient for his surgery. If I've got over the funks, he'll take me there tomorrow. His friend and his wife have to leave for their new home at the end of April, so they'll welcome a quick sale."

"I see," said Emma, thinking that Robert was wise to give Lucy no time for second or third or even fourth thoughts about the desirability of this marriage. In view of Philip's revelations, she felt constrained to hide her qualms and merely said, "And you've got over the funks now?"

"Yes. Suddenly, I feel on safe ground again. You've no idea what a nightmare week this has been for me. Awake most nights, thinking first one way and then another until I wished that Robert would come and carry me off by force as in the wild west stories," she concluded, half laughing.

"Sling you across the saddle and gallop off with you to the Rocky Mountains, you mean? Can't quite see Robert in that rôle," said Emma, who could only treat such preposterous ideas as a joke.

"The trouble is, when I'm with him I have no doubts but, on my own, all sorts of doubts have crept in this past week. About myself, not Robert. I just hate making decisions. But you've helped me put the doubts away this morning."

"Good."

"It will be lovely to leave our gloomy old house behind. It was never a happy one. Phil's been so good to me, making sure that I had a home when I'm sure he would have preferred his bachelor flat."

"Will you keep on your job after you've married?"

"Haven't decided. I don't think so, but Robert leaves that to me."

More agonised decisions, thought Emma, realising how justified Philip's worries about Lucy's mental insecurity were, and determined to offer no more advice. Her own nature was in such startling contrast to Lucy's that she would never be able to judge things through Lucy's eyes.

"We haven't fixed any details like dates yet, but Robert thought early June would give us time to do what we wanted with the cottage. It will only be a very quiet wedding. That's what we both want. Emma, say you'll be my bridesmaid. That will put your seal on it."

Emma could not afford to hesitate although her heart would not be in it.

"Thank you, Lucy. I'll be happy to, if that's what you want."

And Lucy's happy face was her reward.

That evening, she was able to raise the matter of Lucy's future with Miss Arlingham, whose judgment she respected. They were sitting in front of the fire after dinner, for the spring evening was chilly, sharing a pot of coffee. Miss Arlingham was glancing through some old photograph albums.

"Jimmy looked in for tea this afternoon, and we indulged in an hour of nostalgia with the old photographs."

"Can I see them? I feel I know your family from what you've told me. I'd like to see what they looked like."

"Of course, dear. Looking back, they seemed such lovely, innocent days, full of laughter and enjoyment but, of course, one's memory is selective and favours the rosy side. And the war changed everything."

Studying a photograph of a youthful Miss Arlingham in a group of tennis players in the garden, Emma learned that it was taken on the occasion of her youngest sister's eighteenth birthday in 1935.

"My three sisters are in the back row, my brother is the

73

young boy holding the dog and Jimmy is the one with his hands on the shoulders of Margaret, the ten-year-old girl in front, who became my closest friend after the war and who subsequently disappointed us all by marrying Philip's father instead of my brother, who was in love with her. And except for the two children, we all went on to a dance that evening."

"I see what you mean about Jimmy. He was the answer to a maiden's prayer, wasn't he? How much better men looked when they wore white flannels for tennis instead of today's brief little shorts that too often display far from pleasing legs."

"I agree."

"Your brother looks an attractive boy, too. You were a good-looking family."

"My brother and I were very close. Martin was the baby of the family, eleven years younger than me, and I, being the eldest, mothered him. It was a terrible blow to him, though, when Margaret married. They were as good as engaged when Edward Rogart came into her life. A powerful personality. She seemed bewitched by him. A disastrous match. She bitterly regretted it, but divorce or separation was not as easy then as now. But that was all a long, long time ago. Now Jimmy and I are the only survivors of that group."

"You don't think that Lucy is about to make the same mistake as her mother by marrying Robert Bedfield, do you?"

"Has she made up her mind? She was havering, Philip said."

"Yes. She's decided. I feel he's too old for her. Too staid."

"Poor little Lucy. She was always a gentle, rather timid child, and her father shattered what little confidence she had. Robert? He could offer her the security she so badly needs. You take a more romantic view of marriage, perhaps, dear. I'm not against it although, never having married myself, I'm hardly an expert," concluded Miss Arlingham a little drily.

Emma continued to leaf through the album, fascinated by the picture of pre-war life it presented, recognising different aspects of the garden.

"Seeing these, I guess much of your present book is autobiographical."

"In a sense, yes. The period, anyway."

They were interrupted at this juncture by Maurice, who showed great interest in the old photographs.

"Would you be willing for me to write an article on you, Aunt Jessie, with emphasis especially on the old days? I do work for a magazine that I know would jump at it. You're well known back home, you know. I often spot paperbacks of your novels. Readers would love to hear about all this," he said, turning the pages of the album.

"Publicity no longer interests me very much, Maurice, but I've no objection."

"Splendid! I'll start right away by taking some notes."

And Emma escaped as they embarked on a discussion of the past. Although she had told her employer that Maurice did not bother her, she felt uneasy in his presence. The way his eyes dwelt on her sometimes sent shivers of repulsion through her. She avoided him as much as possible and hoped he would soon leave. Her feeling that he was not to be trusted was intensified a few days later, when she found him going through the drawers of Miss Arlingham's desk one evening. She had seen a light under the study door and gone to investigate.

"Can I help you?" she asked coolly, and he straightened up with a jerk.

"Oh, just wanted some stamps. Right out of them. Thought the old lady was bound to have some."

"I look after the stamps. What do you want?"

She held the door of her office open for him and he gave her a humourless little smile and said, "After you."

Pocketing the stamps she took from her desk, he suddenly caught her to him and kissed her mouth at some length before she could free herself.

"Payment in kind," he said. "You're an attractive girl, Emma. Plenty of spirit. I like that."

75

"If you do that again, I'll crown you."

"Don't tell me you object to being kissed. Now what about that evening out? A lively girl like you boxed up here? Not natural."

"I don't think you'd like me to complain about you to Miss Arlingham, would you?"

"You'd look a bit silly, running to her like a child over a kiss. Aunt Jessie's no prude. Her books prove that. She'd laugh at you, my dear."

"Since when has she been your Aunt Jessie?"

"None of your business. We're related. That's good enough."

"Just watch your step, Maurice Braidon, that's all," said Emma vehemently, "and don't go prying into Miss Arlingham's desk without her leave."

"I like you, Emma," he said, laughing. "You're a very welcome challenge in this somewhat sober house. We can have fun."

Speechless, she was looking round for a weapon when Philip's head appeared round the door. He nodded at Maurice, eyed Emma's flushed cheeks and said, "Sorry to interrupt but Aunt Jessica wants the last two pages of her manuscript, Emma. Some alteration she must make before she loses the thread."

"Is that all, Maurice?" asked Emma bitingly.

"For the moment, dear. I'm just slipping down to the village inn for a pint. See that the housekeeper doesn't lock me out, will you?"

His white teeth flashed at her before he went, ignoring Philip, who looked after him with a frown.

"Is that chap being a nuisance or was that an unwelcome interruption?"

She handed him the two pages of manuscript and made no answer.

"I asked a question, Emma."

She eyed him stonily. "My affairs are no business of yours, Philip."

"I see. Lucy has gone off happily to have dinner with Robert tonight. Thank you for restoring her confidence."

76

"I only hope it will work out well for her. Is that all?"

"You repeat yourself. First Maurice, then me."

"Both equally unwelcome."

Silence fell between them for a few moments, then he said slowly, "If anxiety about Lucy made me too forthright last week, I'm sorry. That's sticking in you, isn't it?"

"Not at all. I already knew what you thought about me. I inadvertently came across a letter you had written to Lucy on the subject while we were at college. So your explicit words this time came as no surprise."

"I see. Well, if you're determined to stay up there on your high horse, so be it. I should have thought you might have come down and slugged it out. I'm sure you could use some terms about me that would outdo mine about you."

"I could, but I see no point. I don't wish to have anything more to do with you. Now, if you'll please get out of my way, I'd like to get back to my own room. I've had enough of men for one evening."

"The high horse doesn't suit you, Emma. Not your style. You're a fighter. That icy, injured party act isn't for you."

And at that moment, if she could have laid hands on an axe, she would have used it. As it was, she brushed him aside and slammed the door of her office behind her with a vigour that caused an ornament on the small table in the passage to wobble precariously.

77

10

Assault

For Emma, life at Broomfield took on a chequered pattern as variable as the April weather. Her bruising estrangement from Philip and her more overt suspicion and dislike of Maurice cast the darkest shadows, together with the realisation that Miss Arlingham's strength was fading, despite her vigorous refusal to admit any such thing. It would have helped her to lighten these shadows if she could have shared them, but Lucy was preoccupied with Robert and their plans for the cottage he had bought and Emma saw little of her, while Philip, who was the person she could most usefully have turned to in dealing with her fears of Maurice and her anxiety about Miss Arlingham, was beyond the pale. She would die rather than turn to him for help.

But bright patches emerged in the pattern as well, notably the extension of her involvement in the animal sanctuary and the return of Nick from his travels.

Jill Sandgate outlined her plans to Emma one sunny Saturday morning after they had finished grooming some ponies. Leaning on the gate, surveying her kingdom, she said, "You know I've been giving a few private riding lessons, Emma. Now I've been asked if I can take on a class of disabled children. Some can benefit a lot from learning to ride. It can be physically and mentally therapeutic. I'd love to do it but my hands are pretty full here and I'd need some help. You're qualified to teach, I know. Have you any time you could spare to help me?"

"I'll ask my employer. I think we could organise things so that I could be available a couple of afternoons a week. I'd be very happy to help."

They discussed ways and means, Emma enthusiastic about the idea. She had come to admire this kind-hearted woman who, short of capital, time and space, refused to turn away any victim of ill treatment or neglect, and remained cheerful at all times.

And thus Emma, refusing any question of payment, found herself, with Miss Arlingham's willing co-operation, spending Wednesday and Saturday afternoons giving riding lessons to children whose pleasure and excitement were her reward and whose handicaps pierced her.

It was on account of the children that her anger spilt over at the end of an ugly encounter with Maurice a few weeks later.

He came into her office that morning with a genial greeting.

"And how's my girl this morning?"

"Very busy," said Emma, typing from the manuscript beside her.

"Have you got the keys to the bureau next door? It's locked, but Miss Arlingham put some papers I gave her in there last night, and I want to correct some figures."

"You'd better ask her for them when she gets back from Dilford, then. I don't keep the keys to that bureau."

"And when will she be back? She's seeing her solicitor, isn't she?"

"Yes."

"Why didn't you take her?"

"Because her friend, Jimmy, was going into Dilford and offered her a lift. They're having lunch together afterwards and Miss Arlingham expects to be back early this afternoon. Any more questions?"

"No need to be so officious. She and I have business matters to discuss, that's all. It would have saved time if I could have revised the papers I gave her to study."

And have a snoop through whatever else was in the bureau, thought Emma. He was, she knew, seeking an investment from Miss Arlingham in some business venture. Her employer was, she hoped, too shrewd to get involved, but old people could be vulnerable.

"Oh well," he went on, as Emma continued typing, "it can wait. I'm only trying to do my aunt a good turn, you know."

"I'm sure she appreciates it," said Emma.

Her eyes averted from him, bent on her work, she failed to see the little smile on his face and was taken by surprise when his arms pinned hers to her side.

"You and I need to get together and reach a better understanding, darling. Now seems to be a good opportunity, with the place to ourselves."

"Keep your hands off me," she snapped, but he had pulled her out of her chair and into his arms before she could muster her defences.

His kiss was long and wet and brutal. Sick with loathing, she swung her arm as soon as she was free and hit him across the face with all her strength. He swore and tore at her blouse, his expression now vicious, but Emma was strong and Maurice, red-faced and breathing heavily, was not as fit as he might have been. He grunted as she used her knee and half-winded him, and when she picked up a heavy glass paperweight and threatened him with it, he pushed her aside with shoulder-wrenching force and swore at her again before going out, mopping one eye and slamming the door.

Emma put the paperweight down and sank on to her chair, trembling and enraged. Her shoulder was too painful to move and her mouth was bruised and bleeding. Due to take a riding class that afternoon, she feared she would have to disappoint the children. Jill was already fully committed.

Somehow, with the aid of cold water compresses, she managed to take her class that afternoon and was rewarded for her stoicism by the wide smiles and happy greetings from her pupils. Making up her little group were two spastics, two children disabled in car accidents and two teenagers who had been partially disabled from birth, but who were able to help her a little. Having started with them at a snail's pace, she was now beginning to see improvements in co-ordination and noticeable gains in confidence. But it was taxing work, needing all her concentration, and by the time she waved off the minibus that took the children back to the home, she felt exhausted by the pain of her shoulder and the strains of the day, so that the short walk back to Broomfield seemed to have trebled in length.

In the late afternoon sunshine, the bridal white blossom of the blackthorn lit up the boundary hedge and, as she skirted the little coppice, the first bluebell flowers caught her eye. On the verge of May, the loveliest time of the year, she wished she felt more in tune with it at that moment. The problem of what to do about Maurice weighed heavily. Miss Arlingham seemed to be yielding lately to his efforts to charm her with his solicitous attentions, and Emma was reluctant to trouble her in her present frail state of health, but the prospect of having to fend off Maurice if he persisted was not a happy one. Perhaps he had learned a lesson that morning and would trouble her no more. Shoulders drooping, her head aching and her body sore, pondering the matter, she failed to see Philip's car coming up the drive and forced him to brake suddenly to avoid her. He parked the car by the house and walked back to meet her.

"Sorry, Philip," she said before he could sound off. "I was miles away."

"You . . ." He stopped as he caught sight of her face. "My dear girl, what's happened? Have you had a misunderstanding with a horse?"

She was not his dear girl and she had no wish to go into details of the day's mishaps with him, so she merely nodded and made a non-committal kind of grunt before proceeding towards the house, but when he caught her by the shoulder she cried out in pain and he looked concerned. Her legs seemed to have turned to jelly and when he offered her his arm and said "Hang on," she was forced to accept it.

"Missed lunch today," she murmured.

He made no comment but, when she insisted on going up to her room, not wanting to disturb Miss Arlingham, he helped her up the stairs. Sinking down on the bed, she said, "Thanks, Philip. I'll be all right now."

"What happened?"

"I hurt my shoulder this morning."

"And your mouth. How?"

"Sorry. Too tired to talk."

"Let me look at that shoulder. I can probably help you there."

"No, really. It's nothing much."

"Emma," he said gently. "Will you please stop this childish feud and let me help you – in my professional capacity, of course?" he concluded drily.

When he eased her shirt off her shoulders she was too tired to resist. His fingers were gentle as he explored.

"I can put that right with a little manipulation. Can you stand up with your back to me and just relax . . . ? Relax, Emma. You're as tense as a fiddle string."

"You're not a relaxing person," rejoined Emma, some of her strength flowing back at the challenge.

"Too bad. Forget my objectionable person then, and imagine you're floating on a calm sea. Let everything go limp . . . Good."

She gave a yelp as his hands performed some devilish manipulation, and moved gingerly as he said, "How's that?"

"Better. Oh yes. Much better."

"Good. Just use it normally but don't put any extra strain on it for a few days."

"Thank you, Philip. I'm truly grateful. It was hurting more than somewhat."

"And no fall from a horse accounts for those bruises on your neck and shoulders. Tell me, Emma."

"It was Maurice. He caught me alone in the office and was in an amorous mood. I soon disillusioned him on that score, but there was a skirmish."

He looked at her pale face and swollen lip and his expression was grim.

"Has anything of the sort happened before?"

"Only a verbal nuisance until today."

"Does Aunt Jessica know about this?"

"I didn't want to worry her. She's not at all well these days, Philip."

"I know. And after this assault, you went riding?"

"I was due to take a class for our disabled children. It means a lot to them. I couldn't disappoint them."

She closed her eyes. Someone with a heavy hammer was operating inside her head. Philip's voice was gentle as he said, "Put your feet up while I rustle up some tea and sustenance."

When he returned with a tray of tea and toast, she was lying back in the armchair, eyes closed. He placed the tray on the desk, and poured out two cups of tea.

"Thanks, Philip. I can do with this."

Refreshed by the tea and relieved of the pain in her shoulder, though not of her thumping headache, Emma regarded him warily. He was studying the photograph of Nick on the book-case, his expression thoughtful.

When he looked up and caught her eye, he said, "I'll see that Maurice doesn't bother you again."

"How? I don't want to trouble Miss Arlingham. She seems to be finding his presence more agreeable lately. He's interesting her in some business venture."

"I think she's taking the line of least resistance because she wants to conserve her energy. Her one idea is to finish this book. Nothing else matters. But she won't tolerate any harassment where you're concerned."

"I can cope with him. He came off worst today, I fancy."

Philip shook his head, half smiling.

"However well you take the fight to the enemy, Emma, Maurice Braidon has a mean streak in him and won't fight fair. With a grudge, he could be nasty. That's my impression, anyway."

"Mine, too."

"How pleasant to agree, for once. That being so, there's no question of his remaining here. I'll see to it. Do the dirty work for Aunt Jessica, if need be. Meanwhile, I suggest you lock your door tonight."

83

"It won't lock. The door's warped, I think."

Philip put down his cup and examined the lock.

"I can fix that, I expect, with a few tools. No doubt Joe Bartlow can oblige. These riding lessons you give for disabled children, Emma. Could I come and look on one afternoon? I've two patients who might benefit. I'd just like to see what's involved."

"Whether you think I'm capable, you mean?"

"Not at all. I'm sure you are. I just have to judge whether the particular routines you offer would benefit these particular cases. That is, supposing you can take on any more."

"I'll ask Jill Sandgate, the owner. She was approached to take on this little group from the disabled children's home as an experiment. It's been very successful and we would both like to expand this side of the business, but we're short of space and capital so can't expand much. Come along, by all means, though, any Wednesday or Saturday afternoon, and see what it's all about. In one or two cases the improvement in the children is marked. And they're so happy to be given more mobility."

He nodded and turned his attention to the lock on her door. While he went to find some tools she relaxed, eyes closed, tired. For the first time since they had known each other, she and Philip had met on equal terms today, as allies. It wouldn't last, she thought, but in the harsh circumstances of this long day she had found it comforting.

With the aid of a chisel, a hammer and some oil, he made the lock work before he left her.

"Philip," she said as he was about to close the door, "thank you. And if you have any dealings with Maurice, watch your back."

"I will. Don't worry. He'll be sent packing."

11

Removals

The lane was margined with the white lace flowers of wild parsley, buttercups shone from the meadow grasses and the scent of hawthorn was on the air on that sunny Sunday afternoon as Emma cycled along the lanes to Jean's cottage. The old-fashioned bicycle which she had unearthed from a dark corner of the garage and made usable suited her better as a means of transport in fine weather than Miss Arlingham's car. Her route took her through quiet lanes and pastoral country well away from any main roads and, with the prospect of seeing Nick again as uplifting as the May-time beauty around her, she sped happily along, the breeze in her hair, the sun warm on her face.

Her ring at the door bringing forth no response, she walked round the house and found Jean and Nick at the end of the garden, sitting on a seat in the shade of an apple tree, the abundant blossom of which promised a good harvest. Jean had a book open on her lap and they were deep in conversation, so that they did not notice her for a few moments until Jean looked up and came towards her with a warm smile. Nick's greeting was affably courteous, as usual, and in response to Emma's eager enquiry about his trip, he merely said, "Very satisfactory. And how are you getting on with Jessica Arlingham?"

Somehow, that first meeting after his long absence did not quite fulfil her expectations. She was more aware than ever of his elusiveness behind the urbane charm, perhaps because in his absence her own feelings had intensified and she had ached to see him again. Elegant in grey slacks and a navy blazer, his classical good looks impressed her as forcibly as ever, and her heart was in a state of turmoil which was difficult to hide. But she could not get close to him, break through that friendly detachment with which he seemed to keep everybody at arm's length.

While he and Jean discussed music, she lounged back in her deckchair and leafed through the book they were discussing. *A Life of Love and Music* by Hector Berlioz. Music was a great bond between them, she thought, as Nick brought up some point about a concert of that composer's music which he had attended in Milan. Jean's mother had been a well-known opera singer and Jean herself was an accomplished pianist. Emma wished she knew enough about music to join in the conversation, but her knowledge was not on the same plane as theirs and she contented herself with a cursory glance through the book, on the flyleaf of which was written *For Jean. Nick.* and the date, before letting it rest in her lap while she watched the sunshine flicker through the branches of the apple tree, burnishing Nick's fair hair, casting a dappled pattern across Jean's blue dress.

They were interrupted by the arrival of Diana, accompanied by a white West Highland puppy at the end of a long lead.

"Isn't he lovely?" she said to Emma, who went down on her knees to embrace this lively little body. "Uncle Nick gave him to me at Easter. His name's Benjamin, but Ben will do."

There was an easy, friendly relationship between Nick and his ten-year-old godchild which Emma found a little surprising. 'Good with children' was not a phrase she would ever have thought applicable to Nick Barbury. Perhaps it was because he treated Diana as an equal, with the light touch that bestowed freedom, which paradoxically made the child regard him as infallible.

When Ben, tired by his walk and all the attention, fell asleep in the sun, Diana fetched an essay for Nick to judge. Watching him anxiously while he read it, she looked older than her years, thought Emma. She was wearing navy blue shorts and a white tee-shirt. Tall for her age and slender, her black hair, cut in a pageboy style, framed an oval face with pleasing features and dark blue eyes. Not much of Jean there. A thoughtful, bookish girl who had already decided that she wanted to be a writer. How much this was due to the example of her godfather, Emma could not tell, but Nick obviously thought she had some gift with words for when he had finished reading the essay he said, "Very good, Dinny. Descriptive writing especially good, apart from too liberal a hand with adjectives. Too many makes the picture cluttered. Narrative a bit laboured. Were the Easter holidays so dull?"

"No. But there's not much to say about picnics and going to the seaside for a swim. I mean, they're nice and I like them, but I can't think of much to say about them. Not like describing a walk."

"Well, perhaps Benjamin will bring some action into your life. Dogs and trouble are all too likely companions."

Diana looked at him reproachfully but allowed this somewhat jaundiced view to pass, saying, "Could you tell me how to end it? The last bit doesn't seem right. Seems to stop halfway. I'll send it in just as it is," she added hastily. "But I'd like to know how it could be improved. I don't think our teacher's any good. Only concerned with grammar and spelling."

"Dear me. Well, they are important, but I know what you mean. Let's see. Start from the beginning. Let's have some of these adjectives out of the way, shall we? Too many daisies on the lawn. Got a biro handy?"

Diana sped off to fetch one.

"She shows distinct promise, Jean. You may have the doubtful benefit of a writer on your hands, if you're not careful," said Nick.

"You wouldn't advise her against it, surely?"

"Certainly not. Only the people she lives with. Writers live in a world apart for most of the time. That can be hard for their nearest and dearest to accept."

He spoke with a dry tone that caused Jean to look at him

quickly, but Diana arrived back with a biro and knelt on the grass beside Nick, who set to work on the essay. Emma was sorry that his mood seemed to be disenchanted on that sunny May day, but Jean had read real pain behind his words.

With the two of them immersed in the finer points of writing, Emma went into the cottage with Jean to see about tea. Buttering scones, she wished she could get close to Nick, somehow bridge the distance between them. They had exchanged little more than polite platitudes that afternoon, and that was not good enough after nearly five months' absence. Her opportunity to create a more intimate footing came after tea, when they were left alone in the garden.

"Do tell me about your time in Italy, Nick. Was it rewarding work-wise?"

"Up to a point. I found the university archives in the USA more rewarding. Have you been home lately, Emma? Is all well with the Northumberland clan?"

"I haven't been home since Christmas. I shall be going for the spring bank holiday weekend, I expect. Dad's invited Robert for some climbing in the Cheviots. They discovered a mutual love of climbing when they met last Christmas. Lucy will come, too, of course."

"You don't seem very keen. You were homesick for your moors and hills last time we met."

"Yes. But Mother has invited Philip as well. For some odd reason she seemed to take a shine to him last Christmas. I can't think why. You heard about our Christmas exploits in the fog, I expect."

"Yes. Jennifer mentioned it in her last letter to me. Is Philip such a bugbear? Sounds like a pleasant foursome to me," said Nick blandly.

"Four days in Philip Rogart's company is not my idea of a happy holiday. With Lucy paired off with Robert, I shall be stuck with Philip. I'm just hoping that he's not interested in climbing. Then I can go off climbing with Robert and Dad and leave Lucy with her brother. Lucy's not keen on climbing, though we did quite a bit in our college days. We shall have to see," concluded Emma broodingly. Then she looked up as inspiration came to her. "Nick, come for the weekend with us. Auntie Barbie would love to see you and you disappointed her so much by missing out on Christmas with them."

"Sorry, my dear. I'm already committed."

"Where?" demanded Emma.

"A friend in the Cotswolds," replied Nick with a slightly pained air at such blatant curiosity about his movements.

It was that kind of day, thought Emma unhappily. The man she loved as elusive as a breeze, the man she disliked foisted on her at all turns. It was true that Philip had appeared in a more kindly light over the affair of Maurice Braidon, who had quitted Broomfield that weekend. When she asked Philip how he had managed to rid them of the pest, he had said, "Only by a few words to Aunt Jessica. She did the rest. No row. Splendid diplomacy on her part. I wasn't needed. A regretful turning down of his business proposal because her accessible money was little and the rest was tied up for the two charities to whom she was leaving her estate. A little hint that the decorators would be descending on Broomfield shortly to paint and paper the spare room, and Maurice accepted defeat and moved out with ill-concealed coolness."

It had been an unpleasant episode. Miss Arlingham had merely expressed her regret that Emma had been bothered by him and said no more on the matter. Since then, Emma had been on guarded terms with Philip, but she winced at the prospect of having him at home under the same roof for four days with herself his obvious companion, since Robert and Lucy were paired and, moreover, so obsessed with their plans for the cottage and the wedding that Emma felt invisible in their company. She hoped Robert would be able to concentrate on climbing instead of curtains and carpets when with her father, leaving Lucy to bore Philip with those domestic topics. She intended to be out on the hills – if not with her father and Robert, then by herself. Her mother, she thought uncharitably, could talk books with Philip.

Dwelling on these disconsolate matters as she cycled back to Broomfield through the dusk, she realised that at the heart of her discontent lay the failure to get close to Nick. She had set out with such happy anticipation that afternoon, only to find that the gap between them had, if anything, widened. Always courteous, affable, he kept her at arm's length when she had so much warmth to give him, such an eager desire to share his mind and heart. She was holding out her hands, but he refused to see them.

The first faint stars were appearing by the time she cycled up the drive of Broomfield, and the air was fragrant with the scent of the wallflowers at each side of the porch. But, for once, she was hardly aware of the beauty of that warm, tranquil evening with the fresh new growth of May-time all around her. It seemed to mock her dashed hopes. She felt tired and close to tears.

Jean and Nick lingered in the garden as the light faded, for the warmth of the day still held. Diana had gone to bed with a book, and Jean had brought out a tray of coffee and biscuits and placed it on the wooden seat between them. They were quiet, at ease together. They had always been able to be silent together and feel companionable. Small talk had never been needed. It was Nick who broke the silence as he sipped his coffee.

"Do you know the Cotswolds, Jean?"

"Darrel and I spent a holiday in Burford one spring. Good walking, lovely little villages. The heart of England. I liked it. Darrel found it a little too cosy, I fancy. He preferred wilder, more remote places for holidays."

"I'm thinking of spending a few weeks exploring those parts. I'm tired of my hotel base. Time I found a permanent place of my own. The Cotswolds appeal."

"You've decided to settle in England, then?"

"Yes."

"The Cotswolds will take you a long way from the Rainwood clan. They will be sorry."

"Near enough," he said with a little smile.

She would miss him, she thought sadly. Miss him badly. He had brought warmth back into her life after six years of grief that had lain like a frost on her spirit. As though

90

sensing her sadness, Nick went on gently, "A change of scene can help with the grief of bereavement. No reminders to stab you. Wouldn't you have found it easier in new surroundings, my dear?"

"Perhaps. But I was too numbed to do anything about it. I'm not very brave, you know. Not a fighter. You have your work. So rewarding. That must help you to get over past losses."

"Yes. It was partially the cause of them, though. I haven't discussed it with anybody else, and don't intend to, but I'd like you to know the facts."

He leaned forward, his hands clasped together, and seemed to be studying the grass at his feet before he went on.

"For the first few years our marriage was all that mortals could wish, but Debbie wanted a child. When pregnancy continued to elude her, we sought medical investigation. It turned out that Debbie couldn't have children. I won't go into the gynaecological details. Some malformation. It didn't affect me so much. I'm not wildly paternal. But Debbie was deeply unhappy. She was a person who, perhaps more than most, needed to be needed. My work absorbed me and, although we were happy together, a child would have sealed it for her. But she found fulfilment elsewhere," concluded Nick grimly, and fell silent.

Jean said nothing. A blackbird nearby broke the peace of the darkening garden with shrill warning notes. A cat prowling nearby, perhaps. Nick's profile was etched against the pale sky. She knew he found it difficult to speak of such personal, intimate things, this man who never wore his heart on his sleeve and had such charming and impenetrable defences against the eyes of the world. When he went on, his voice had the detachment of a lawyer.

"You've heard of my French friends, the Rochelles, I believe. Marc was an old friend. A musical family. They ran a music school in the manor house which had been the family home, but which they could no longer afford to keep up just as a home. Marc was a fine violinist and teacher, his young sister a cellist. Debbie had a part-time job there on the admin. side during the first years of our marriage. Marc married a year after us, to Yvonne. Her health was delicate after their first child was born, and Debbie gradually slipped into being nursemaid to the baby. When the third of Marc's children was born, Debbie was spending more time with the Rochelles than in her own home, and loved the children as though they were her own. I was glad that she'd found some compensation for her own childlessness and I suppose I should have foreseen what would happen. But my work took me away quite often, and Debbie was too indispensable to Yvonne to come with me. I didn't force the issue because I've always believed in personal freedom, anyway. Possessiveness is an evil."

"Marc was not proving a good friend in all this," said Jean.

"Looking after his own convenience and, of course, glad that Yvonne should have such devoted help with her family as Debbie provided. She was never strong and died a few years ago of heart failure, leaving Marc with three children aged four, two and six months. I don't need to say what happened. Marc's need was greater than mine. That's all."

"I'm so sorry, Nick."

"Well, I should have remained a bachelor, as I always intended. I'm not cut out for the domestic life; perhaps no writer is."

"I think Debbie was too young for you, Nick. When you're young and in love, you expect so much. It would have been better if she had had interests of her own to balance yours, but personal relations were always more important to Debbie than anything else."

"No use tracking back. No blame attached. Just the way the dice fell. I couldn't have foreseen Debbie's infertility, nor the effect it would have on her. It all ended in a very civilised manner. Let's just call it a misalliance, and leave it at that," he concluded drily, and Jean knew he would say no more.

She laid her hand on his shoulder for a moment, then said gently, "Come in and have some music. What would you like me to play?"

"I'd find Bach consoling. Detached, orderly, a rebuke to the chaotic nature of life. But not such a favourite of yours, I know."

"Bach it shall be," she said as he picked up the tray and followed her into the cottage.

It was nearly midnight before he left. She walked out to his car in the lane. The moon had risen and the garden took on a magic quality in its pale light, with the fragrance of the while lilac tree by the gate filling the air.

"If I don't see you again before you leave, I hope you find what you're looking for in the Cotswolds, Nick."

He took her hand in his for a moment, then stooped and kissed her cheek.

"You've made my return to England much happier than I expected it to be, my dear. Thank you."

"We're such old friends, Nick. We share so much. No question of thanks. You'll keep in touch, won't you?"

"Of course. Haven't I always?"

It was true. Even during the years when he had been absent in France, his letters had come at regular intervals and he had never forgotten Diana's birthday and Christmas presents. Theirs was a special relationship forged all those years ago in Ireland. As she watched the tail lights of his car disappear round a bend in the lane, she hoped it would not fade away in his absence, but she had a premonition that he had been saying goodbye.

12

Losses and Gains

"Gone away?" said Emma, dismayed. "He didn't say anything about it last weekend. Only that he'd be going to the Cotswolds for the spring bank holiday. That's two weeks away."

"He's going house-hunting."

"For himself?"

"Who else?" said Jean, tugging some bindweed from the flower border.

"Well, I do think he might have told me. His sister's hoping to persuade him to stay some time with them in Northumberland this summer."

"Nick's his own man."

Emma knelt down beside Jean and pulled a piece of grass out of the border in a rather half-hearted manner.

"How long have you known Nick, Jean?"

Jean sat back on her heels and considered.

"Must be all of seventeen years."

"He's not easy to know, is he? Not really know, I mean."

"It takes time."

"And if he finds a house in the Cotswolds, I suppose he'll do a complete vanishing trick."

"Oh, I dare say he'll turn up now and again. His work fills his life. Writers need to be able to work without distractions."

"They need to be human, too."

Jean smiled at the note of exasperation in Emma's voice.

She hadn't an earthly chance of getting near Nick. The last thing he would allow would be any involvement with a young girl who was in love with him, giving her false hopes. But Emma looked pale and unhappy, and she felt sorry for her. Hoping to turn her to happier prospects, she said, "I expect you're looking forward to going home for the bank holiday weekend. You look a little tired. Can do with a rest, I guess."

"It has been a bit hectic lately. Miss Arlingham is going all out to finish her book. She's obsessed with it. We've been working all hours. And Mrs Bartlow's been down with flu so I've been stepping in on the housekeeping front, too. Not that I mind. I like to be busy."

"Well, you can relax in that lovely Border country."

"Wrong company for relaxation. I really don't know why Philip chose to accept my mother's invitation. Lucy and Robert are so wrapped up in each other, they won't want him, and he and I get on as well as hare and hounds. What with coping with him and the endless talk about the wedding from Lucy and Robert, I'd sooner be typing Miss Arlingham's book."

"And when is your friend's wedding?"

"Four weeks' time. My bridesmaid's dress is the colour of pink ice cream and I look a right mess in it."

"I doubt that."

"I wish I felt happier about this marriage. Robert's nice enough, but years older than Lucy and so stolid. I really expected her to have more sense than to tie herself down to domesticity before she'd enjoyed any freedom. We'd made such plans. I just can't see the attraction in Robert, but I think Philip engineered it."

"Nobody can judge for others, Emma. The most unlikely marriages prove successful and the most promising often come to grief."

Silence fell between them for a few minutes as they worked along the border on that sunny Sunday afternoon. Jean sat back on her heels and watched a furry bumble-bee work furiously on the flowers of a foxglove, buzzing into each pink bell as though there was not a second to spare. Emma was

95

tugging at a dandelion which had no trouble in resisting her efforts. Lifting her head, giving up the struggle for a moment, she said, "I wish I'd known Nick when he was young. What was he like? More forthcoming then? Didn't he bowl you over with those looks?"

Jean smiled, thinking back to that summer in Ireland when she had first met him.

"He was witty, delightful company always, with a lively intelligence that charmed us all. Before our stay in Ireland was over, he was our very good friend. More light-hearted than now, but otherwise not much changed."

"But you didn't fall for him?"

"I fell for another."

"But he stayed your friend."

"Yes. Mine and Darrel's. You're pulling up my treasured ligularia instead of the dandelion."

"Sorry," said Emma gloomily.

"Cheer up. Try and get on better terms with Philip and enjoy your holiday in the Border country. I rather like the little I've seen of him. What is it about him that you dislike?"

"Everything. Or nearly everything."

"Oh dear," said Jean, laughing. "I'll say no more. Except that I resented an awful lot about the man I married before I fell deeply in love with him. So people can improve on acquaintance."

"Maybe," said Emma, jumping up. "Sorry I'm a misery today. Must be sickening for something. Shall I dig up that corner you want to clear for some summer bedding? Might work off the blues that way."

"Of course. I've a beautiful new stainless steel fork in the shed. You can christen it."

But what Emma was afflicted with was the pain of unrequited love for Nick, thought Jean, watching her retreat to the toolshed in the far corner. That could hurt so much when you were young. There was no consolation she could offer.

Cycling back to Broomfield early that evening, Emma felt

the loss of Nick like a chilling wind, for she faced for the first time the fact that he had never allowed her to get within arm's length of him and now never would.

Pushing the aged bicycle up a steep hill, she turned aside at the top and followed a footpath through a narrow belt of woodland which brought her out to an open stretch of grass and a fine view across the Weald to the North Downs. Sitting on an old tree stump, she gazed across the wide expanse of English countryside in all its May-time freshness, and acknowledged defeat. It was foolish to pine for the unobtainable. That dream was over. She must bury her rejected love and get on with living without it.

By the time she pushed her way back through the wood and resumed her journey she had said goodbye to Nick, but twice on the journey she had to brush tears from her eyes and, in spite of all admonitions to herself to display more backbone, she viewed the coming holiday weekend with all the enthusiasm of a visit to the dentist. Philip Rogart, as well as foiling her plans for going into business with Lucy and manipulating a marriage for Lucy which had more or less broken up their friendship, was now, by his presence, spoiling the prospect of going to the home and countryside that she loved. And, just then, she had no spirit to fight him. Nick's departure had undone her.

As though to cap her unhappy state, the old bicycle decided that it, too, was giving up, for with a clang and a squeak, the chain came off, depositing Emma in an ungainly sprawl at the side of the lane with the bicycle on top of her. Investigation confirmed that the machine would function no longer, but she had reached the boundary of the donkey sanctuary. Manhandling the bicycle through the little wicket gate, she left it propped against a tree and walked on through the trees which skirted the field where the donkeys grazed. She had no wish to see Jill or anybody else just then, and was dismayed to see Philip chatting to her on the far side of the field. Slipping back into the shadow of a hazel tree, she waited. She watched Jill return to her cottage, and Philip turn back towards Broomfield. Giving him five minutes, she moved, only to find him leaning on

97

the gate to the field, rubbing the nose of an emaciated donkey. She tried to slip back but he saw her.

"Don't run away, Emma. I was hoping to find you. Aunt Jessica didn't know where you were but thought you might be here."

"I've been with Jean all the afternoon."

"Walked all that way?"

"No. Cycled. The bike gave up the ghost just as I reached here. I've left it on the boundary. I'll get Joe Bartlow to fetch it with the trailer tomorrow but I think it's beyond repair."

"As it's a relic from Aunt Jessica's youth, it's high time it was scrapped." Then he registered her pale cheeks and reddened eyes. "Were you hurt, Emma?"

"No. Only a grazed arm."

She leaned on the gate beside him, not because she wanted to linger, but she felt in need of a breather. The tumble had shaken her more than she had first realised.

"I've just had a word with Jill Sandgate about taking my two patients for a course of riding lessons. She thinks she can fit them in. Your hands are too full with your young class, she says."

"Yes. The little ones need so much watching."

"I was very impressed with the way you handled them when I was here yesterday. They seemed so happy and confident. You have a way with children, Emma."

"They're so brave, and quite lacking in self-pity. It's very rewarding to see them make progress; spastics getting control of convulsive muscles and growing in confidence. I've become very fond of them."

"Well, they certainly like you. Their faces when you arrived were a revelation."

"It's a great treat for them to be mobile with the ponies."

The donkey pushed against Philip's arm, craving attention.

"Poor old Nicholas Nye," said Philip, stroking the grey nose.

Emma glanced at him swiftly.

"Do you know 'Nicholas Nye'?"

"Nicholas Nye was lean and grey,
    Lame of a leg and old,
More than a score of donkey's years
    He had seen since he was foaled."

As though hearing a hawk pour forth the song of a nightingale, Emma gazed at him in astonishment.

"I would never have expected poetry from you."

"No?" He looked at her with amused eyes.

"No."

"You forget that Aunt Jessica had quite a lot to do with my upbringing. I spent most of my free time at Broomfield when I was a kid. An escape from my own less agreeable home. And Aunt Jessica saw to it that my literary education was not neglected. *Peacock Pie* was a favourite source when I was five or six. She was an excellent reader of verse. For that, and much else, I've reason to be grateful to her."

"I suppose that's why you hit it off so well with my mother," said Emma thoughtfully, perceiving a reason for the rapport which had puzzled and not altogether pleased her. "She's always loved poetry and is a bookish person."

"Yes. She rather hoped you'd go for a literary career of some sort. She said it was a toss up between seeking a job in a publishing firm or physical education. Two extremes."

"At our college for physical education you were able to take subsidiary courses and I chose literature, so had the best of both worlds. Somehow, though, I never fancied being shut up in an office. I haven't made much of a mark in either."

"Early days. Hope this weather holds for the holiday weekend. Lucy and Robert are going in their car because they want to take an extra day to visit Robert's parents. Can I pick you up at midday on Friday? That's the earliest I can get away."

Emma surveyed the prospect gloomily. As though sensing her lack of enthusiasm, he said drily, "You could travel with Lucy and Robert, of course."

"Two's company. You name a time. Miss Arlingham will agree, I'm sure."

99

"Say one o'clock, then, after an early lunch. What's wrong, Emma? You look unhappy. You haven't hurt yourself with that fall, have you, and are nobly suffering in silence?"

"No. Just a bit tired. Did some digging in Jean's garden this afternoon."

"Is Nick back from his travels yet?"

"Been and gone again, probably permanently. Jean says he's aiming to buy a house in Cotswold country and go to ground there."

"An elusive character."

"Very. I must be getting back. Goodbye, Nicholas Nye," she said, with a pat for him.

Philip walked back with her. Nearing the house, he broke the silence and startled her by saying, "I don't believe you're looking forward to the weekend, Emma. I guess I'm the jarring factor. Shall we try to put past friction behind us and reach a better understanding?"

"We can try," she said pessimistically, "but I'm not in a very receptive state just now."

Immediately she had said the words she regretted revealing so much, but it was too late. Philip picked her up quickly. "You and Nick Barbury?"

She nodded, bereft of words but too unhappy to be able to hide her feelings from his searching eyes.

"Well, I could offer bromides like 'It would never have worked, you know,' but it hurts and seems like the end of the world, so I'll only say that distraction is the likeliest help, so why not turn your attention to finding something tolerable about me so that we can enjoy the holiday weekend?"

"I'll try," she said ruefully, then had to laugh at his wry expression. "After all, a man who can quote from 'Nicholas Nye' can't be all bad," she concluded with a twinkle in her eyes which had him laughing, too.

That day of surprises, pleasant and unpleasant, had yet one more to enact, however, for on stepping into the hall of Broomfield, they were brought up short by the astonishing sight of Jessica Arlingham and her old friend Jimmy fox-trotting to the cracked strains of an ancient record and singing:

"I can't give you anything but love, baby,
    That's the only thing I've plenty of, baby."

Jimmy's passable baritone entwined with Jessica's reedy soprano.

Philip's eyes rested with incredulity on the old wind-up gramophone on the oak chest, from which these strains emerged.

"Come on, you two," called Jimmy. "See what you can do."

Emma beat down her first reaction of alarm at the threat these activities might pose to Miss Arlingham's angina, for she was singing and smiling so happily that admiration for her spirit demanded co-operation and, turning to Philip with a smile, Emma went into his inviting arms and they circled the hall in imitation of their elders but without adding to the choral effects.

"Oh!" exclaimed Miss Arlingham as she sank down on a chair, puffing a little. "How that brings back memories! I can even remember the red-haired Scottish lad I danced it with at Chrissie's twenty-first. What was his name? Stuart something. He had an eye for Chrissie and left me flat in the middle of the dance when she appeared. I was deeply humiliated."

"Such goings-on," said Philip, shaking his head. "And where did you find that ancient gramophone?"

"In the loft. Jimmy went up there to fetch some old magazines for me and found the gramophone and a pile of old dance records. We've had a lovely time playing some of them. Funny how old tunes bring back such memories. The age of innocence. Another world."

"And that night," said Jimmy, "I missed the last bus home and had to walk three miles. None of us sported cars in those days."

"And then the war came and we all got scattered, and somehow never came together again in the same way. Now we're two lone survivors, Jimmy. Belonging to a different era, aliens in today's world. But I won't think about that. Thank you for taking me back to the old days, my dear. Now for some refreshment. Emma, you've hurt your arm."

"Just a graze. It's nothing. I parted from the bicycle in an unfriendly manner."

But Miss Arlingham was not to be put off thus lightly and demanded a full explanation.

"That old bike ought to have been scrapped years ago. You should have taken the car. I'll see about a replacement for you, dear. Now go and wash that arm while I see to some supper. You two young people must be hungry and I'm parched and so is my dancing partner, I'm sure."

But Emma, noticing Miss Arlingham's pallor and slight breathlessness, said quickly, "Give me your orders, and I'll see to it after I've cleaned up."

Emma found Philip in the kitchen before her, brewing coffee.

"I've carved some ham, if you'll make the sandwiches. Any more damage come to light?"

"Just a bruise or two. I was lucky. Must say I'm peckish."

"A reassuring sign. I left Jimmy and Aunt Jessica, if you'll believe it, way back in time again, waltzing to a number called 'Three o'Clock in the Morning'. If we don't stop these capers with some food and drink, we shall be carrying Aunt Jessica off on a stretcher."

"How they live in the past! That's all they have, memories."

"Aunt Jessica has her writing."

"But that's all in the past, too, now. *No Sad Songs* is her last book, she says, and it's set in the pre-war days of her youth. I think it's very good."

"Nostalgia is in fashion now."

"I think your aunt is one of the bravest people I know. She has so much pain from the arthritis in her hands, as well as angina, and yet she never complains or gives in. I don't think I want to live to be very old, do you, Philip?"

Philip surveyed the coffee beginning to bubble in the Cona while he gave this question some thought. Then he surprised her by saying slowly, "I might, with the right person to share it."

They gathered round the big bay window in the sitting-room as light faded in the garden and Miss Arlingham switched on a standard lamp. They spoke little, a quiet reflective mood prevailing. Tiredness washed over Emma as she sipped her coffee and looked out at the garden. The creamy flowers of an elderberry tree on the far side of the lawn stood out in the dusk, while nearer at hand a white rose rambled through the branches of a half-dead tree, a pale ghost against the dark yew hedge. Through the window came the scent of pinks. A lovely summer night. If she were not so tired, she would like to be out there, savouring it, but the events of the day had exhausted her and the ache in her heart for Nick undermined her.

She looked away from the garden to find Philip's dark eyes studying her thoughtfully. He had been kind to her that day, she thought. Unexpectedly sensitive about Nick. It was one of the rare times when they seemed to have met on equal ground. That was a small grain of comfort in a day of broken dreams and wounding rejection.

13

Border Country

The weather for the bank holiday promised to be fine, and Emma hoped to find some ease for her hurts in walking and riding in the country she loved so much, but she viewed the weekend before her with mixed feelings as she settled herself in the passenger seat beside Philip for the long drive north. His suggestion that they should try to reach a better understanding was one she viewed with caution, so deep had been the divisions between them, and the unhappiness over her rejection by Nick hovered like a grey cloud over the family reunion which she would normally have looked forward to with pleasure. She would have to mask her unhappiness at home, for she shrank from any probing into that sensitive area. But with Philip, Robert and Lucy their guests, and doubtless much coming and going of members of the clan, that should not be too difficult.

Philip, when driving, obviously liked to concentrate on the job in hand and said little. He was a good driver, unfussy, not given to explosions of anger at the lunacies of other drivers, as was her father, and Emma herself on occasion. He had an empathy with his car which inspired confidence, and she was able to relax with her thoughts. There had been a time when the mere presence of Philip Rogart aroused in her a state of tension, had her on her toes, ready to take on any challenge. This was no longer so. Her feelings towards him now were confused, ambivalent, wary, but Nick had so dominated her thoughts during the past months that her war with Philip had in any case been pushed into the background.

Philip diverged from their route to lunch at a small country hotel which had been recommended to him.

"Monica knows it well and vouched for its good food and pleasant surroundings."

Monica? Emma dragged her thoughts back from Nick. Of course. Monica Ringford, the glamorous young woman at Miss Arlingham's birthday party last Christmas. The long-standing friend of Philip, viewed with some aversion by Lucy. He had never mentioned her before in Emma's hearing and she wondered just what the relationship was, for Monica Ringford had a sex-appeal that had rippled all round that table and would do so in any company. Emma remembered Nick's cool grey eyes dwelling on her once, with that faint little smile with which he so often seemed to view the world.

Monica's taste in hotels, however, proved faultless. Tucked away at the end of a long, narrow drive, it looked across a meadow golden with buttercups, and was backed by low woodland. Its white walls and black timbers were softened by a rambling wistaria whose age was proclaimed by the thick, tortuous trunk.

They both chose cold salmon and salad for their main course and, waiting for this while she sipped a glass of orange juice, Emma, with thoughts in her head of Monica, tried to see Philip through the eyes of other members of her sex, for she had been so influenced by her intense dislike of him that she had only registered the calm assurance of his manner, the measured assessment of his dark eyes, the infuriating authority of that firm mouth. Now she had to concede that with his crisp black hair, tall, lean build and pleasing voice, he would be attractive to her sex, provided his cool assumption of authority as of right did not antagonise others as it did her. But beside Nick's fair, handsome elegance and witty, but completely unmalicious, tongue, Philip appeared a dark tyrant. Nick would never dictate to others. Would charm with his sensitive understanding. Would lift your spirits with his ready tongue and light touch. And would, she concluded with a sigh, leave you aching for more of his elusive company.

"Robert tells me that your father is planning to climb the Cheviot with us this weekend. Lucy's thinking of going, too. Is she up to it, do you think?"

"We had some climbing instruction in our college days, and Lucy was nimble enough but not really confident. Nor all that keen."

"That's what I thought. But it's like getting the peel off an apple to separate her from Robert these days."

"Yes. I haven't set eyes on her for weeks. When I phone, she's usually out."

Something in her tone caused him to study her thoughtfully, then he said, "My sister has always needed a firm support to cling to. At first I provided it, then at college you were made for the job. Now it's Robert. Don't feel hurt. Your friendship still means a lot to her."

But Emma knew that Lucy had changed direction, permanently. For the first time it occurred to her that Philip had, after all, been right in opposing their business partnership, deeply though she had resented his interference. If the riding school had run into trouble, great or small, Lucy would have worried and wilted. Responsibility all too easily overwhelmed her and decisions were difficult for her. Emma felt she could have carried her but not prevented her from worrying ineffectually at every little difficulty. That much she had learned in the months since they had left college. But she could not bring herself to express these thoughts to Philip, admit that he had been right. Mr Right needed no bolstering, she thought darkly, and merely observed, "It's only natural. Engagement and marriage usually break up friendships."

"Shall you join the Cheviot assault party?"

"I don't know. I've done it several times. I want to reclaim my pony from my uncle's care and do some riding."

There was no way she was going to be paired off with Philip this weekend, better understanding or not. She wanted to nurse her wound of severance from Nick by herself

106

in her own way, and was still annoyed with her mother for inviting Philip without consulting her, an annoyance which was not soothed when in reply to her complaint that evening, her mother said cheerfully, "Three's an awkward number, darling. I didn't want you to feel odd man out, and Philip's such a very pleasant addition to the party."

"Why should I feel odd man out in my own home?" demanded Emma, wiping a dish with unnecessary vigour.

"Then let's say that I enjoy the company of Philip Rogart, and leave it at that, shall we?"

And when her mother adapted that tone of voice, there was no more arguing.

"Over to you, then," said Emma, and left the field. But things did not work out at all in the way she had planned.

The weather being fine, the Cheviot party set off early the next morning, Emma's father driving the hatchback car to their starting point. At the last minute Candy, the young retriever, leapt into the car and was reluctant to be dislodged.

"Let her come," said her father, impatient to be on their way, and Emma and her mother waved them off down the drive.

"I hope your father will remember that he's in his fifties and not his thirties. That last bout of flu left him well below par," said Joyce Vurney as they turned back into the house.

"Don't worry. He's got two strong young men with him. I'll take Floss with me," added Emma as the old retriever nuzzled her hand. "You won't be wanting your old jalopy, will you, Mummy?"

"No, dear. I'm going to have an orgy of cooking today so that there's plenty of cold food for the rest of the holiday and I can be free to enjoy myself."

"Should I stay and help?"

"No. Only room for one woman in a kitchen. Enjoy your day and give my love to Jenny and Joel. Tell them we're looking forward to the party on Monday evening."

"Who's going to be there?" asked Emma, who viewed

107

this family get-together with less than her usual friendly attitude. The one member of the family circle she ached to see would be absent.

"Kit and Giles and the boys. And Jenny has her sister and brother-in-law staying with her. She's very disappointed not to have Nick to complete the family reunion."

"Nick's a loner," said Emma briefly.

She enjoyed the peace of that day, riding through the country she knew so well, lingering by a burn to watch trout, eating her sandwiches on a heather-covered hill, watched uneasily by two sheep with large curly horns, heavy fleeces and black stockings. Floss lying beside her, nose on paws, large dark eyes watching her, sharing a sandwich. And there she finally came to terms with her lost love, and rode slowly back to her aunt's home, Foresters, which had once been her home when her parents were in India, and where she was always welcomed with love.

All had not gone as peacefully with the Cheviot party, however, for Emma arrived home that evening to a tale of mishaps.

"That silly dog went chasing after a rabbit down a steep drop on to an insecure ledge and couldn't get up or down. Robert and Philip somehow fetched her up, your father slipped and fell trying to help, and the result was a sprained ankle for him, a damaged knee for Philip and a painful return to base. They should never have taken Candy. That dog has a genius for getting into trouble," concluded her mother.

"A good thing both Philip and Robert are experts where damaged joints and muscles are concerned. Not serious?"

"No. But it's rather spoilt the weekend for your father and Philip. Lucy's retired with a headache, having feared imminent death for Robert."

Emma, seeking the injured parties, found her father in the sitting-room, his foot propped up on a stool, a drink beside him, reading the paper.

He looked up at his daughter with a rueful grin.

"In trouble again. I'm afraid your mother's right. Time I gave up these strenuous activities."

"Mother's always right," said Emma drily.

"Annoying, isn't it? But what should we do without her common sense?"

"Do you intend to give up climbing, then?"

"Of course not."

"Quite right. What's a sprained ankle, after all?"

"Mm. I feel a bit guilty about Philip, though. If it hadn't been for him, I'd have gone down further than Candy. Now I've clipped his wings for this weekend."

"Not to worry. I'll try to salvage the holiday for him."

"Do that, dear. Nice to have your bright face about the place again. Did you have a good day? Where did you get to?"

Going in search of Philip a little later, feeling more concerned than she had revealed, she found him sitting on the seat by the stream at the end of the garden, two walking sticks beside him, his leg outstretched. The sun was setting and, in the dappled shade beneath the old apple tree, she had not seen him at first.

"Hullo, there. So sorry about this, Philip. How bad?"

"I shall live," he said, with a little smile. "Robert's trussed me up. Nothing that a few days' rest won't put right. Just a confounded nuisance. All this lovely country to explore, and I'm immobilised."

She sat down beside him, guessing from his drawn face that he was in some pain.

"You saved my father from what might have been a serious fall."

"We didn't turn out to be very expert. A bit of a scrambled exercise. But we could hardly expect Candy to understand our instructions."

"She's a mad creature. Floss is so obedient and intelligent, I don't know why her offspring is so crazy. Will you be able to drive, do you think?"

"A bit uncomfortable for a day or two, I guess."

"I'll chauffeur you around and show you the country. It's the least I can do when my family has managed to spoil your holiday."

"I accept your kind offer with thanks. I can see you prefer

109

me with my wings clipped," he said, with an amused gleam in his eyes which she ignored.

"Tomorrow we'll take a picnic and go north to the River Coquet valley – glorious country. It'll madden you not to be able to walk, but at least you'll be able to see the possibilities."

Afterwards, Emma saw that weekend as a watershed, when she finally relegated her love for Nick Barbury to a hinterland of dreams and entered a new phase in her relationship with Philip Rogart, which was nothing if not realistic and had nothing to do with dreams.

Robert and Lucy elected to drive to the coast the next day and Emma was standing by her father's car, studying a map, when Philip limped up, still needing two sticks. She held the door while he got into the passenger seat. Before she drove off she handed him the map and pointed out the route.

"I think, Emma, you've got me where you want me," he said with a little smile.

"I have to make the most of any advantages that come my way. I don't get many. I expect you hate being driven."

"I prefer to drive. I'm sure this is going to be for the good of my soul."

"I'll try not to give you too many shocks."

"Don't let me spoil your enjoyment. You're looking very pleased with yourself this morning, and most attractive."

His eyes dwelt approvingly on her grey trousers and cherry red sweater and Emma, unused to compliments from him, merely smiled briefly and put the car into gear.

It turned out to be a surprisingly happy and relaxed day. Gone was the tension which Emma usually felt in his presence. Keen to show him the country she loved, she found him an appreciative companion. She parked the car off a narrow road high above the river valley, and found a clearing in the heather nearby with a handy rock for a back rest.

"How does it feel?" she asked as Philip lowered himself gingerly on to the travelling rug.

"Not at all bad. What a view!" he said, gazing down

110

the tree and heather clad slopes of the valley to the silver thread of the river winding along far below, the folds of the Cheviot Hills in the distance.

She left him studying the large-scale map of the area and set off down a narrow track to the river. Dawdling by the water, she looked up once to find him evidently watching her, for he waved. Scrambling up afterwards, she arrived back puffing a little, and more than ready for their sandwiches.

After their lunch they fell silent, wrapped in the peace and quietness of the hills around them. A faint rustling in the leaves of a silver birch tree nearby, the call of a distant curlew and nothing else to break the silence. When, after some time, Emma turned to pick up the binoculars to watch a hawk hovering high over the valley, she found her companion asleep. He lay on his side, one leg curled beneath him, the injured one stretched out. He was a quiet sleeper and looked younger with the dark, challenging eyes hidden, the faint breeze stirring a lock of hair on his forehead. She guessed that the knee was more painful than he had let on and had given him a restless night. She watched him with oddly confused feelings. A greater contrast to Nick would be hard to find, in looks, temperament and character. Nick melted her, Philip challenged her. But the nature of the challenge was changing. She removed a leaf from his hair and he woke.

His eyes held hers for a moment, then he said, "Didn't mean to fall asleep on you. In this beautiful place and in such agreeable company, what a waste! I apologise."

"It was only a short nap. I've been watching a hawk. Not you. One up in the sky."

"A pity my dove-like qualities are quite lost on you," he observed lazily, his eyes challenging.

But for once Emma ignored the challenge and took up the map, pointing out a river valley to the south of them.

"This is where I got to yesterday, starting from Auntie Barbie's home, which is on the outskirts of Benbury, this village here."

111

"And that's where we're gong to a party tomorrow evening, I gather."

"Yes. A family party. Auntie Barbie's sister and brother-in-law and their children, and the Coalvilles from Castleton. Aunt Christine Coalville is Auntie Barbie's cousin and the Castleton estate is five miles or so down the river valley, about here on the map. It's a tree nursery and timber-growing estate. So you see, it's all very cosy."

"Do you miss all this – the country, the family connections – down south?"

"Sometimes. But going away to college loosened the ties a bit and I wanted to be independent, not get sucked into any of the family businesses. I always love to come back, though. I used to find the family connections a bit irksome, especially the Coalville cousins, but I was thinking only yesterday about Miss Arlingham, alone in that big house this holiday weekend, and I felt there was a lot to be said for belonging to a large clan, even if some members were a pain in the neck."

"Mm. Nick Barbury doesn't seem quite to fit into the scenario."

"He's a loner. Much to Auntie Barbie's regret. But he's attached to the clan in his way. Has been very kind to certain members in the past, I'm told. I guess he doesn't need other people to the same degree. More self-sufficient. That's a kind of strength, I suppose."

"And you're too warm-hearted for your own good, perhaps."

Surprised at his words, she was silent for a few moments, then said, "People, friends, do mean a lot to me. I could never be happy on a desert island."

"It's growing less painful? Nick?"

"It was always a lovely dream, I guess. Too bad that Dad and Candy between them have clipped your wings, Phil. There are so many glorious walks round here."

"If I come up here in the autumn, will you show them to me?"

"With a map, you won't need me."

"But would enjoy it much more. Will you?"

"Yes. Are you going to be able to drive home on Tuesday? You could stay on for a few days, you know. You'd be most welcome."

"Thank you, but I've a full book of appointments for Wednesday. I'll manage. The knee's a lot better today."

"We could share the driving, then. If you can bear to."

"Thanks. I'll be glad of some back-up. In spite of all, we don't make such a bad team, Emma," he said with a smile as he ruffled her hair.

"I'll have to watch you. I can't think this dove-like state of affairs will last."

"Might be rather dull if it did. I'm all for variety. This has been a splendid day," he added as she began to pack up the picnic basket. "Thank you, Emma."

Walking the dogs round the garden late that evening, Emma was glad to be alone with her thoughts. The last of the daylight of the long summer day was fading and a full moon was glinting through the branches of the old ash tree beyond the orchard. The pungent scent of catmint nearby lingered on the air. A dog barking in the distance was the only sound as Candy and Floss nosed their way busily over the damp grass and disappeared in the deep shadow of the hedge.

Sitting on the seat at the end of the garden, she pondered on the unexpected enjoyment she had found in Philip's company. They would try to reach a better understanding, he had said, and she was aware that he had probed her to good effect that day without revealing much of himself. Did people matter to him too, or was he, like Nick, basically a loner? She thought not. He was, after all, very much involved with Miss Arlingham, and obviously had a care for Lucy although she had first seen this as objectionable interference. And he was in a caring profession. Perhaps that could account for the authoritarian side of his nature that had so antagonised her in the early days. If you were dealing with patients in pain, worried and disabled, such confident management would be reassuring and thera-peutic. Understandable if he carried that over into his

113

personal life. Understandable but annoying and needing to be resisted. But she was cautiously revising her earlier unfavourable judgment of him, and she owed him a credit mark that day for keeping her thoughts from Nick until this moment, and that was a good thing, she concluded as she called the dogs.

On the following day, the weather holding, she drove her parents and Philip to a riverside haunt where her father proposed to do some fishing, which was about all he was good for with his sprained ankle. Lucy and Robert had opted for the coast again. Philip's knee was sufficiently improved to allow him to limp along the river bank in search of a base for some sketching. Emma went with him.

"I didn't know that sketching was a hobby of yours," she observed as they settled themselves close to a little hump-backed bridge, beneath which the shallow water bubbled and rippled its way over a stony bed.

"Don't have much time for it these days. I find it a pleasant relaxation."

She took out her book while he worked, but couldn't concentrate on it and idly watched the water and the acrobatic skill of a dipper, bobbing and curtsying on a small rock in midstream. The gentle murmuring of the water lulled her into a dreamy mood so that she was surprised to find that an hour had passed when Philip laid his sketch block aside.

"That's good. That's very good," she added, sitting up and studying it. "Have you studied art at some time?"

"Went to an art school in the evenings for a year before I went to medical school. Never good enough to take it up seriously. Just an enjoyable hobby."

"Have you ever exhibited?"

"No. Not in that class. At least, Monica has occasionally put one or two of my things in her exhibitions of local artists when she's had space to fill."

"Is she a practitioner herself or merely an exhibitor?"

"She wouldn't like the term 'merely'," he said with a little smile. "No. She's not an artist herself but she knows a great deal about art. Her father and her grandfather before him

114

owned that gallery. It's well known. They mount stunning exhibitions."

"I must keep my eyes open and go to one."

"They're well advertised in the *Dilford Herald*."

They fell silent for a few minutes. Emma wondered just how close was the relationship between Philip and Monica Ringford, but she could hardly ask if Lucy's fears about them were likely to be realised.

"That old chap looks a likely candidate for Jill Sandgate's sanctuary," said Philip as an emaciated donkey emerged from some bushes lower down the river on the opposite bank.

A boy appeared with a switch and ushered the donkey back. As they disappeared, Emma said, "There are always more candidates than she can take. Jill's short of space and cash. She's not rich and finances it all herself. The riding lessons don't amount to much. She has such a soft heart but is so unbusinesslike."

"Yes. I gained that impression."

"There's quite a lot she could do to raise funds for such a good cause. Seek sponsors for the donkeys and let them take an interest in their choices, have open days and jumble sales. I've made suggestions but she just smiles and says she'll think about it, but I know she won't. She works so hard and she's not young. I wish I could give more time but of course Miss Arlingham and her writing are my first concern."

"You're happy working for my aunt, aren't you?"

"Yes. I like the literary work and she's taught me a lot, in more ways than one. And I find her memories of the twenties and thirties, and her family life at Broomfield, fascinating. She just brings it all to life for me."

"I never thought for one moment that you'd take to the job so happily and do it so well."

"You made that very clear at the time. You had a very unfavourable view of me, all round."

"I've learned better. Some aspects are decidedly appealing," he said, with a wicked gleam in his eyes, as he took her in his arms and kissed her.

A little confused, for he had taken her completely by surprise, she looked up at a face that expressed a friendly affection guaranteed to melt any resistance, and she said, "The view from this side has changed quite a bit for the better, too. That's not to say that I expect the sun to keep on shining."

"Oh, I think we'll weather the storms well enough, don't you?"

"Could be," she said lightly and stood up, holding out her hand. "Come on. If we don't get back soon, my parents will have wolfed all the lunch."

On his feet, he laid a hand on her shoulder.

"Thank you for staying with me and making this holiday so enjoyable for me, Emma."

"A pleasure."

"Unexpected?"

"Yes."

He laughed, and they made their way back along the riverside path in such a leisurely manner, stopping to watch a kingfisher halfway, that Emma's prophecy was not far short of the truth, the picnic being well under way by the time they arrived.

The family party that evening rounded off the weekend on a cheerful note. Philip, perforce an onlooker when dancing ended the evening, was standing, glass in hand, surveying with interest the more active members of this large family gathering when a soft voice beside him said, "I'm afraid we're a bit overwhelming en masse. What my brother Nick calls a family barney, to be avoided at all costs. I do hope you haven't found it a bit much after the damage which I'm told my brother-in-law inflicted on you."

He turned to meet the dark brown eyes of his hostess and said, "No fault of Mr Vurney's, I assure you. And only trivial damage. To tell you the truth, I've rather enjoyed being taken under Emma's wing and basking in her sympathy."

"Dear Emma. She's always had a very soft heart for injured parties. Even when she was a tough, belligerent

116

four-year-old, always scrapping and giving as much as she got and more, it was the one sure way of softening her into a less intractable frame of mind."

"You had the onerous task of looking after her at that age, I believe."

"Yes. Her parents were in India and Emma was left in the care of Joel's mother. When she had a stroke, Joel had to take over and hired me. My good fortune. Emma rescued me from a state of deep depression after a personal tragedy, and that was how I met Joel."

Philip's eyes were on Emma, dancing the Gay Gordons with one of the cousins, her fair hair swinging, her full jade green skirt flying as she was twirled vigorously by her partner.

"I guess she was a handful."

"A strong-minded child with a tremendous zest for life and uncompromising in her likes and dislikes. Utterly lovable, exasperating and exhausting."

"I don't think she's changed very much."

"Well, one doesn't. The basics, I mean. But she's grown up this year. I must confess I was a little worried about her going off to the south, away from us all. She's a little too impetuous for her own good, and I hoped my brother would keep an eye on her. He has sent me reassuring letters now and again, though, and I gathered she was in good hands."

She was studying him thoughtfully, a slender woman with a sensitive face, fading hair and a gentle poise which he found appealing. Philip sensed a need there for further reassurance.

"I don't think you have any cause to worry, Mrs Vurney. Emma is a sturdy character and has struck up a real friendship with my aunt, who has grown very fond of her and has her welfare at heart."

"And for whom, I believe, you hold a watching brief?"

"My aunt is an old lady and very much a lone survivor. Actually, no blood relation but my godmother, and aunt by adoption when I was very young. A close friend of my mother's. I owe her a lot and do what I can."

She nodded and gave him a warm smile as her husband came up.

"Come on, Jenny. Show these youngsters that you can dance the Gay Gordons with the best of them. Excuse me, Philip."

And Joel Vurney took his wife off to join the dancers. Philip's eyes returned to Emma's laughing face as she danced with zest, fleet-footed as a fawn, twirling and weaving with easy grace in the hands of an equally skilful young partner. If she was suffering from the pangs of unrequited love, he thought, she was hiding it very well.

14
Wedding Day

The wedding of Lucy and Robert took place on a hot day at the end of June. Lucy's wish for a quiet wedding had resulted in a modest assembly at the church and at the reception, which was held in Dilford's only hotel, where a buffet lunch was prepared for them. Lucy looked pale and slightly nervous in the church and Robert as stolid and composed as usual.

Emma, more reconciled to this marriage than had at one time seemed possible, did not, however, enjoy the occasion as wholeheartedly as she would have wished. For one thing, she was a little worried about Miss Arlingham, who had been unwell the previous day but had insisted on attending the wedding after a bad night. And in a more trivial vein, she felt at a disadvantage in this too ingenuous, shrimp-pink dress which had been Lucy's choice, and she was not helped by being subjected to an amused scrutiny by Monica Ringford at the reception.

"Dear me! How very rosy you look, Emma."

Emma screwed her lips into a smile and made no reply. Monica was looking the acme of elegance in an ice-blue silk suit, beautifully cut, with the uncluttered simplicity of high cost. On this hot day, she looked as cool and attractive as chilled wine in a crystal glass.

"Our little Lucy looked a little overwhelmed, I thought," she went on, and sipped her champagne as she scanned the assembled guests with a somewhat bored air.

Cat. Patronising cat, thought Emma, as she said sweetly,

"Lucy has never enjoyed being in the limelight, but she has no qualms today."

"Quite. A very satisfactory arrangement all round, I'm sure. Not least for Phil." Her expression changed and she turned a dazzling smile on Philip as he came up to them. "How very impressive you look in morning dress, Phil! I can only presume that Robert's father took his out of the moth balls in which they were incarcerated half a century ago."

"Not meant to be a fashion show, my dear. Can I fetch you ladies anything more to eat?"

"No, thanks," said Monica and tucked her hand in his arm. "Come over here, Phil. Something I want to show you. A little gem of a drawing tucked away among the monstrosities on the wall behind the buffet. I can't read the artist's signature. Perhaps you can. I'd like to know."

And she led him away, leaving Emma seething. How could he put up with such a proprietorial attitude? Or perhaps he enjoyed it. As she was decidedly peckish, she followed them across the room to the buffet and helped herself to a selection of canapés until, with a full plate, she sought Miss Arlingham, who was tucked away in a corner on the far side of the room, hoping to persuade her to share these tempting items. Failing in this, she sat down beside her, concerned at her pallor.

"You're in pain."

"It will pass. I've just had one of my pills. It's easing already. Amazing what a little nitrate will do."

And as Emma stayed with her, taking in some food to offset the slightly dizzying effect of champagne, Miss Arlingham's face relaxed and she viewed the gathering with more interest.

"Robert's parents seem kindly people and have taken Lucy to their hearts. I'm very pleased and relieved. Lucy's not well armoured for this world. She needs a safe harbour."

"Philip's pleased about it, too. Removes the responsibility from his shoulders."

"He's been very good to his sister. But no doubt he'll

be glad to move from that gloomy old house and live an independent life again, knowing that Lucy's in good hands."

"Is that what he's planning to do? Sell the house?"

"Yes. Nothing to keep him there now. A house of unhappy memories. I shall leave as soon as Lucy and Robert go, dear, but don't let me take you away."

"There won't be any junketings afterwards. Robert's parents will be off to London, where they're spending a week's holiday, and there's no point in lingering. Always an anticlimax when the bride and groom have left."

"Yes. And not exactly a sparkling gathering, with so few young people. Your family would produce livelier wedding assemblies, I expect."

And so Emma took her leave of Philip immediately after Robert had driven Lucy away to an unknown destination.

"I'm taking Miss Arlingham home now, Philip. She's exhausted. You'll be winding up the proceedings soon, anyway."

"Yes. I'm driving Robert's parents to the station. I hope you've found this a happy occasion after all, Emma," he said, studying her thoughtfully.

"Yes. I'm not anxious any more on Lucy's behalf."

"Good." He laid a hand on her shoulder at this tacit admission that he had been right about this match, and added with a smile, "We can reach agreement sometimes, you see."

"Mr Rights can become very irritating, you know."

"Too true."

"Here comes the feline Miss Ringford," said Emma tartly. "I'm off. She sheathes the claws for you, I believe."

"I'll look in later on to see if Aunt Jessie's all right," he called as Emma melted away.

When he appeared at Broomfield early that evening, Emma was able to reassure him. Miss Arlingham had refused to retire to bed and they were enjoying an evening of nostalgic music.

"Will you join us?" she asked.

"Sorry. I'm already committed."

121

When she went to the front door to see him off, she was not pleased to see Monica Ringford in the passenger seat of his car. As they drove off down the drive, Emma felt an irrational desire to relieve her feelings by doing something violent. As far as she was concerned, this wedding day had been a flop, and she would like to have walked across to the stables and galloped one of the horses across the heath to rid herself of this fractious mood. But she could not leave Miss Arlingham in this frail state and would have to try to soothe her sore feelings with 'Moonlight and Roses' and other numbers of that ilk played by the dance bands of Miss Arlingham's youth. And never was a programme less suited to her present mood than that.

It was on a hot, sultry day towards the end of July when Miss Arlingham handed the last few pages of her book to Emma and sat back in her chair with a deep sigh.

"That's it, Emma. The best I can do."

"And now you can take a rest while I type a fair copy."

"I feel an odd mixture of relief and regret when I finish a book. Relief to be able to relax the concentration, and regret to lose my characters and their world. Particularly this time, when their world was really the world I once knew and enjoyed. And perhaps more than anything, I feel drained at the end."

"Wouldn't you like to take a holiday? I could hold the fort here and get on with the typing."

"Too old to drag up my roots, dear. But I can rely on you, I know, to see the book through now."

"We'll have a grand celebration on publication day."

"Perhaps."

But, as Emma had feared, the old lady let go with her task completed. It was almost, she thought, as though she had decided to drift away. She spent a lot of time sitting in the garden in a dreamy state, serene and passive, and blessedly free of the arthritic pains and angina attacks which had overshadowed her life for long past, and which she had endured with such fortitude. If the garden was peopled for her with the shadowy figures of the past, it was the happy hours she was remembering, for her mood was both gentle and tranquil.

It was at a chance meeting with Jean Brynton in Dilford the following week that Emma heard news of Nick. They had met in the library and adjourned to a nearby café for coffee.

"I'd planned to ride over to your cottage tomorrow," said Emma. "I've been a bit tied down lately with Miss Arlingham going all out to finish the book. It's done at last, and she's resting now and letting me take over."

"Do come. I've a bumper crop of raspberries this year. Would you like some?"

"Rather."

"Good. We'll have a picking session tomorrow."

"Have you heard from Nick lately? Is he back?"

"No. He's found a house near Burford. He won't be coming back here except for a flying visit some time soon to pick up some books and papers he left with me."

"Oh. We shall miss him."

"Yes."

"More than he'll miss us, I dare say," said Emma wrily, and turned to discussing books.

Driving back to Broomfield, she found herself in a vaguely unhappy mood of uncertainty. She seemed to be standing on shifting sands. Things, friends, were slipping away from her. Lucy was lost to her, Nick gone, and Miss Arlingham fading fast. Philip had put his house up for sale. Whether he saw his future with Monica Ringford she could not tell, but change was in the air all round and seemed to be leaving her in a no man's land. Even the future of the donkey sanctuary was now threatened as Jill Sandgate's financial position grew steadily worse.

As she turned into the drive of Broomfield, a few leaves drifted down from the silver birch tree by the entrance.

In this hot, dry summer, the trees were beginning to take on autumnal colours earlier than usual. And her own mood just then was autumnal, too.

15

Summer Fête

On Saturday morning a week later, Emma was helping Joe Bartlow load up his van with pot plants and cut flowers destined for the Dilford fête when Mrs Bartlow came hurrying out of the house carrying a briefcase.

"Oh, Emma, Miss Arlingham says would you be kind enough to drop this briefcase in at Mr Rogart's surgery in Dilford as you'll be driving past it on your way to the fête? He left it behind last night, and it contains some X-rays he'd collected from the hospital which he wants before Monday."

"Right. Hasn't Joe got a fine show for us? I reckon we'll get a load of customers at our stall today," said Emma, surveying with pride the pots of pelargoniums, fuchsias and less familiar greenhouse plants. The fête was an annual affair held in aid of local charities and it was obvious that for Joe it was a challenge to his horticultural skill that he thoroughly enjoyed. He was fretting a little that morning at the heat that threatened to beat the previous record of that hot summer.

"Hope we'll be able to find a pitch in the shade," he said, giving a last sprinkle to the fuchsias.

Bumping along the lanes to Dilford, Emma sat in the back of the van, keeping an eye on the two buckets of cut flowers, steadying the pots when necessary.

Philip's surgery was in a tall Victorian house on the fringe of the town. Joe parked the van nearby and Emma ran up the steps, through the open door and into a room on the left marked 'Reception'. A matronly woman with greying hair, horn-rimmed spectacles and a motherly expression was behind the desk, booking an appointment for an elderly woman with a voluble tongue.

"It was so good of Mr Rogart to see me today. I know he doesn't usually treat patients on Saturdays. I just couldn't have gone away with my back so bad. A slipped pelvis, Mr Rogart says. It feels better already. At least I can walk more or less comfortably. But I'll have to take things carefully while I'm away. Wouldn't it happen just now? I'm determined not to miss out on the holiday, though. Do you know Corfu, Mrs Roland?"

With great tact, Mrs Roland extricated herself from a lengthy discussion about Corfu and escorted the patient to the door, where renewed thanks for seeing her on Saturday were countered with a smile and an assurance that Mr Rogart had to come in to treat another case and not to worry but enjoy her holiday.

As the receptionist turned to Emma with an apologetic smile, Philip came in, wearing a white coat and looking preoccupied.

"Hullo, Philip. Your briefcase."

"Many thanks. Careless of me to forget it last night. It's going to be a scorcher for the fête."

"Yes. Will you be coming?"

"Some time this afternoon. See you there. Hullo, Jim," he added as a tall, sunburned young man came in. "Go right through. I'll be with you in a minute."

He saw Emma to the door and thanked her again for bringing the briefcase.

"Working overtime, Phil?"

"Yes. Don't reckon to work on Saturdays unless it's something urgent."

"That young man who's just arrived didn't look in any sort of trouble. Very fit, I'd have said."

"One of our county cricketers. A bowler with a niggle in his back and a one-day match tomorrow. I've known him for a long time. Have a successful day."

Rejoining Joe, she found him removing a blemished leaf

125

or two from a dahlia. Joe was a perfectionist where his plants were concerned.

Their stall was a rich tapestry of colour by the time they had finished setting it up, with the bunches of dahlias, antirrhinums and delphiniums forming a framework for the pot plants, and they did brisk business from the start, Emma handling the money, Joe wrapping the goods.

Although they started off with the stall in the shade, the sun had reached it by early afternoon and Emma pulled on a white linen floppy hat to shield her face, for her fair skin was apt to burn in such fierce heat. They snatched a lunch of sandwiches and a cold drink from the refreshment tent in turn and Emma kept a supply of mineral water to hand, which was soon lukewarm.

By tea-time they had sold everything but two pots of ferns and a bunch of flame-coloured dahlias, and Emma was wilting a little in the heat. Looking across the field, the sight of a fair head made her heart jump. Could it be Nick? No, of course not. Too tall. She searched the crowd for Jean, who had said she would probably come, but could not see her. Then two familiar figures came into sight. Philip and Monica Ringford. With them was a slight, dark, clean-shaven man formally dressed for such an occasion in a light suit and a panama hat. They were heading her way.

"You've had a good day, then, Emma? Only the remnants left for us," said Philip.

Monica nodded coolly and as she made no move to introduce her companion, Philip did so for her. His name was Pierre Darmont and he was a friend of the Ringfords over from Paris to spend the weekend with them. He removed his hat, gave Emma a flashing smile and a little bow.

Monica, dressed in a peach-coloured sheath and white high-heeled sandals, looked delicious and stood out from the motley crowd drifting about the field like a lily in a cabbage patch, making Emma conscious that her navy linen trousers, blue and white nautical-style top and floppy white hat, while suitable for the job in hand, did not give her morale the boost which she needed in the presence of the glamorous Miss Ringford.

"Come along, Monica, do your duty," said Philip. "I'll take the ferns, Emma. They'll cheer up my reception area. Monica, what about the flowers?"

Monica regarded the dahlias with a singular lack of enthusiasm, but could not get out of it. She probably thought they were vulgar, thought Emma, less than careful in wrapping them so that they dripped a drop or two on Monica's dress, and she promptly handed them to Pierre.

"It's so hot, I thought of driving Pierre to the coast and having a meal at the Cliff-top Hotel, Phil. Might get some cooler air there. Won't you come with us?"

"Sorry, my dear. I really must get down to some paper-work this evening."

Monica frowned, then turned a dazzling smile on Monsieur Darmont.

"Well, we'll be off then. It's a grand view of the coastline on top of the cliffs there, Pierre, and I think even you will find the food there more than passable. So long, Philip."

And ignoring Emma, she turned away. Pierre smiled at Emma, murmured goodbye and went off, bearing the dahlias like a torch before him. They looked out of place as they walked towards the car park, as though they had strayed from a royal garden party into a tatty market-place, for the stalls were now empty or half-empty, there was a good deal of litter about, and a dwindling crowd drifting round, clad in all kinds of casual gear deemed suitable for a heat wave.

"Well, I doubt whether Monsieur Darmont will have gathered a favourable impression of an English summer fête. He looked a bit dazed, I thought. Do you know him, Phil?"

"I've met him only once before. He's an art dealer the Ringford Gallery does business with, I gather."

"He looks as though he might be nice to know if Monica would let him off the chain."

"Where's Joe?"

"He went for a cup of tea."

"You look a bit tired. Can I hold the fort while you get a cup yourself? Or can I fetch you one?"

"Yes, please. I can tot up the takings while you're gone. I think we've done well."

He came back shortly, balancing two cups of tea on a tray, and perched himself on an edge of the stall while Emma sat on an upturned box.

"That was heavenly," she said when she had drained the cup. "Now I'd better clear up before Joe gets back. He looked whacked out."

"Yes. I saw him in the tent. Told him not to hurry. You sit there. I'll clear up."

And he set to, gathering up the surplus wrapping paper, collecting the litter, stacking the boxes and buckets. There were times, thought Emma, when she was happy to let Philip take charge, a state of mind which she would have found unbelievable a few months ago. His dark, hawkish face pleased her as she sat watching him.

"We've made seventy-five pounds and fifty pence," she said triumphantly.

"Well done."

"Do you know how to look after those ferns?"

"I'm not an expert on pot plants, but I've no doubt my Mrs Roland is. She has a greenhouse. I know that because the roof blew off in the January gales and she was very distressed at the damage to her plants. The ferns will be in good hands. That's tidied everything up, I think," he added, straightening up.

"Thanks a lot, Phil. I'll just pay this in to the treasurer, then we can get going."

"You know, you look very trim and attractive to the eye in that outfit. You've got the right figure for trousers. Structurally, you're near perfect, you know."

"Really? Praise indeed! You are speaking from a professional point of view, I take it."

"That as well," he said, and laughed at her expression.

Not knowing quite how to take him, she picked up her bag, which held the takings, hooked it over her shoulder and collected the tray with their empty tea-cups.

"I'll drop these in on my way," she said briskly.

When they finally left the site, only a few remaining bargain-hunters remained. At the entrance to the car park, Emma looked back again to see if Jean had turned up late, but there was no sign of her. Knowing the retiring nature of her friend, Emma guessed that she had, after all, settled for a deck chair and a book in her shady garden.

But Jean had, in fact, been otherwise engaged.

16

One Enchanted Evening

Jean looked at herself in the mirror with a critical eye. The long black skirt and frilly white blouse were all that she had been able to produce by way of evening wear for this unexpected event in her quiet, secluded life. She had lifted her hair back from her face and wore the silver drop ear-rings which had been Darrel's last present to her. She was thinner these days, and the skirt had needed a rapid adjustment to fit her slender waist. She sighed. It was the best she could do, but she looked rather faded. Her lack of confidence was boosted somewhat, however, by her daughter's words when she saw her.

"Gosh, Mummy! You look super!"

"Thank you, darling. Have you packed your case?"

"Yes. There was no need for me to have to spend the night at the Jordans, though. I'd have been all right here on my own."

"Yes, but rather lonely for you. I shall be late back. And you like Brenda Jordan. You'd rather spend the evening there than on your own, wouldn't you?"

"I suppose so. Do you like opera, Mummy?"

"Very much. Especially the one we're going to hear. *The Marriage of Figaro.*"

"Seems silly to me."

"You'll probably learn to like it one day. My mother was an opera singer, as you know, and I expect you've enough of her genes to come round to enjoying it."

"Did Daddy like it?"

"Yes. He loved music, as I do."

"Why do you have to dress up?"

"It's all part of the glamour of Glyndebourne. A lovely opera house in a beautiful country setting and delightful gardens to walk in during the interval, so it calls for evening dress just to do justice to it all. The trouble is, I don't have such finery these days, and Uncle Nick gave me too short notice to buy anything."

"You look super," repeated Diana, then ran to the window as she heard a car. "It's Uncle Nick."

As she bounded down the stairs to let Nick in, Jean smiled. Her daughter's penchant for Nick never waned. It was typical of him to have phoned her casually the previous day to say that he had tickets for Glyndebourne and would she be free to accompany him. Nothing would have kept her from such a treat, and she felt happy and rejuvenated at the prospect before her, so shorn had her life been of all such enjoyments for years past. With Nick, dearest of companions, and a kindred soul where appreciation of opera was concerned, the success of the evening was assured.

They dropped Diana off at her friend's house on the far side of the village and drove through Sussex lanes drowsing under the August sun. Avoiding all main roads, there was little to disturb the peace of the early evening apart from an odd farm tractor trundling along. Hawthorn berries and rose hips were plentiful in the hedgerows, and along the margins of a field of ripe corn there were glimpses of poppies. Sheep grazed in fields which the summer drought had rendered honey-coloured, and cattle sought the deep pools of shade cast by the trees. And over all the chequered pattern of that peaceful countryside presided the smooth lines of the whale-backed downs.

Pondering on the beauty of the Sussex countryside and wishing that Nick had chosen to find a home among the rolling downs, she said, "What made you choose the Cotswolds for your home, Nick?"

"I've always liked the feel of that part of England. The villages. The rivers. And I've some connections at Oxford."

131

"Tell me about the house you've found."

"Typical old Cotswold stone house, leaded light windows, not large, an acre of ground. A couple of miles from the village. Good views, and well off the tourist track. Needs a great deal done to it. I'm seeing the architect and builder about it at the end of the week."

"So this is a very brief visit. A lovely way to celebrate your find, though. Thank you for including me, Nick dear. You know there's nothing I enjoy more than opera, and with the added beauty of Glyndebourne itself, what more could one ask? I've only been here once before, to a performance of *Falstaff* with Darrel."

"And *our* last visit to the opera was to *The Ring* cycle at Covent Garden. Years ago in our salad days. Remember?"

"As if I could forget."

She fell silent, her thoughts travelling back those sixteen years to the early days of their friendship and the fraught time of Darrel's courtship, which had blossomed into such a deeply happy marriage.

"Well, Mozart will be far lighter than Wagner, more suitable for a celebration," said Nick as he swung through the entrance to the opera house.

For Jean the whole evening had an enchanted quality and she felt like Cinderella transported to the ball. Pushing back any sadness at Nick's imminent departure, intoxicated by the music, Nick the ideal companion to share it, she strolled through the garden in the interval, her arm in his, singing some of the music, and felt happier and more alive than for years past.

"Delectable Mozart," she said. "I'd like to feel he was enjoying this performance up there in heaven, where he surely must be. Such genius must be immortal."

"You look as though you're up there among the stars yourself tonight."

"I am."

And driving back beneath a moon-washed sky, both singing snatches of the opera now, some of the enchantment stayed with them.

At the top of a hill before the last dip down to her cottage,

Nick pulled over to the view-point and they stepped out of the car and stood looking over the fields to a glimpse of the sea through a gap in the downs, shining in the moonlight like a small mirror. Now and again, in the distance, the headlights of a car appeared and disappeared along the coast road. The air was still and warm.

"Jean, have you ever thought you might marry again?"

"No. When Darrel died, half of me died too."

"The other half – is that lonely?"

"Yes. But I've learned acceptance. Or perhaps just given in to it. I'm not much of a fighter."

"But tonight you've come to life again."

"Yes. Thanks to you."

"I suppose you could say we're both survivors. I've been thinking while I've been away that we might be able to salvage something worthwhile together. We've been friends a long time, Jean. I've always been very fond of you. I proposed to you once, in Ireland. Remember?"

"No woman ever forgets a proposal. And it was a very nice one."

"And very gently turned down because your heart was already given to Darrel."

"And we were very young and romance was in the air. And a lovely setting for a proposal, that sandy bay in Kerry. I seem to remember reading a poem to you about roses and love."

"We weren't as down to earth then as the young are today, I fancy. How did it go?

> The red rose whispers of passion,
> And the white rose breathes of love,
> O, the red rose is a falcon,
> And the white rose is a dove.

Can't remember the rest. Very pretty sentiments. But a lot has happened to dampen our confidence since then. We still have a future, though, Jean. I think we could be happier sharing it. So, for the second time of asking, my dear, will you marry me?"

"I hadn't anticipated this, Nick. You seemed so set against marriage after your break with Debbie."

"Yes. But this is different. We know each other so well. Share interests. Won't expect from each other more than the other can give. If, after Darrel, you can't contemplate it, I'll understand. You said half of you had died. I'd be grateful for the other half. But Debbie said I was too immersed in my writing to give anybody more than a small bit of myself. You may feel the same."

"When you're young and in love, you demand and expect so much. And Debbie always wanted to look after people. To be needed. It was never a suitable match, Nick, and circumstances worked against it, too."

"Perhaps you need time to think it over," he said, as she lapsed into silence, gazing across the countryside.

She turned then.

"No, Nick dear. There are many kinds of love. We've shared a loving friendship for many years. It's proved durable. I've not known happiness for a long time, but I know I shall be happy sharing your ivory tower. And although I'd never foreseen this, it seems entirely natural now that we should travel on together."

And he took her in his arms then, saying, "It does to me, too."

17

Letters

Emma stopped typing and stood up, stretching her stiff shoulders, for she had been working non-stop since nine o'clock and it was now almost lunchtime. She walked to the window and looked out across the sunny garden. Miss Arlingham was sitting in the shade of a cherry tree, the newspaper on her lap. As Emma watched, the paper slid off her lap on to the grass at her feet. The old lady had fallen asleep.

She returned to her desk, stacked up the pages she had typed and put the cover on her typewriter. In the hall she met Mrs Bartlow.

"Lunch is just on ready. Perhaps you'd fetch the missis, Emma? I don't want to leave my custard."

The dry grass crackled under her feet as she crossed the lawn. The border was full of colour, with sunflowers, marigolds, phlox and fuchsias vying with each other. There was a drone of bees on the lavender as she passed and she stopped to watch a large bumble-bee disappear to forage for honey in a purple foxglove. Under the cherry tree, a leaf had fallen on Miss Arlingham's grey hair. Then something in the angle of her head caused Emma to quicken her steps. But with her hand on the thin shoulder, she realised that there would be no calling Miss Arlingham to lunch for she had died, as she would have wished, in the garden of her memories.

There was only a small gathering at the funeral of Jessica

Arlingham for she had lived a reclusive life for some years past.

Saddened and still unable fully to realise the finality of the loss, Emma found Philip a strong support as he took charge with a quiet competence that did not entirely mask the extent of the loss to him.

They were the last to leave the graveside. As they turned away, he put a comforting arm round her shoulders for a moment. Ahead of them, Jimmy was walking slowly down the path to the lych-gate, his shoulders bowed, such a lonely figure that Emma's eyes filled with tears as she watched him, and Philip, seeing this, took her arm and said, "Come along, dear. No sad songs, remember. She wouldn't wish it. She wanted to go, and went, as she had hoped, in her own home, peacefully. If we grieve, it's for ourselves."

"Yes."

"Tea's waiting for us at Broomfield. After that, you and I have business matters to discuss. I need your help. So brace up."

Emma sniffed and nodded, and was glad of his arm as they walked from the church to his waiting car.

In her office early that evening, Philip was brisk.

"I saw Aunt Jessica's solicitor yesterday. She discussed her will with me a few months ago and gave me her instructions. She left two letters with Mr Saltburn. One for me, one for you. Here's yours."

"Thank you. I'll read it later."

"You've nearly finished typing her book, I believe?"

"Yes. Another week will do it."

"She left you to deal with the publishers, check proofs and so on. And she wanted this dedication."

He handed her a slip of paper on which was typed:

To Emma, my dear young friend and helper.

This threatened Emma's control as she gulped, then collected herself, but could find no words, merely giving him a nod and a quavery little smile.

"She left you a small legacy. She hadn't a great deal to

leave. She's taken care of the Bartlows as far as she was able. Has left Broomfield to me. I'll leave this copy of her will with you. Happily, Aunt Jessica was a businesslike woman and has left precise instructions. As you'll see, she wants you to have all her old papers and photographs if you would like them. She told me that you had a feeling for the past. Might even like to write about it one day. Might you?"

"We talked about it once. I said I liked the idea of writing a book for children set in the twenties, using her experience. She made that period live for me. Broomfield has become peopled with ghosts for me, too."

"Well, there'll be a load of stuff to sort out. Aunt Jessica was a great hoarder. That about wraps it up, I think."

Emma was silent for a few moments, toying with her biro. The realisation that her job here was coming to an end was just dawning on her, bringing with it a hollow aching feeling of uncertainty about the future. She looked across her desk at Philip, to find him studying her thoughtfully.

"You've found a buyer for your house, Lucy says. Where will you move to, Philip? Here, to Broomfield?"

"I've no definite plans. Completion date for the sale of the house isn't until the end of November. No hurry. I think, once you've got the book off, you should take a holiday, Emma. You've been looking tired lately. Aunt Jessica drove you pretty hard, I guess, to get the book finished. A couple of weeks' holiday are due."

Prior to getting her dismissal notice, she thought, for there would be no job for her here now that Miss Arlingham had gone. She was surprised at the desolation she felt at this prospect. Lucy had said that she wouldn't be surprised if Philip joined up with Monica Ringford now that he was free of family responsibilities. "But you know Phil," she had said. "Never gives much away."

She put her biro down and tidied some pages of typescript, saying, "Yes. I'll probably go home."

"And now I'm going to take you out to dinner. You look washed out and in no mood to get yourself anything to eat here."

He drove to a quiet little restaurant in Dilford, where the good food and Philip's gentle mood with her went some way to restoring her morale. He talked of the holidays he had spent with Jessica when he was a child and she had a holiday cottage in an Exmoor village. Of a holiday in Switzerland with her which she had given him for his twenty-first birthday present.

"I may have been unlucky with my father, but no child has ever had a better godmother than I."

"A consolation for not having any children of her own, perhaps."

"She was very devoted to my mother and helped her endure an appallingly unhappy marriage."

"She thought your mother should have married her brother. They seemed set that way until your father came on the scene."

"It would have been better for Lucy and me, particularly Lucy, if she had. You've been more fortunate in your family, Emma. It shows in your confidence. Lucy was shattered by it."

"But in a safe harbour now."

"Yes. But the damage will always be there. A chancy business, life. To be born into a happy, secure home gets you off to a flying start, I guess."

They were at ease with each other that evening, meeting on equal ground, and Emma was aware for the first time how much she would miss him when she left Broomfield. An awareness that amazed her, so greatly had her feelings changed towards him.

They were both in a reflective mood on the journey back to Broomfield. Philip left the car at the entrance and walked up the drive with her. In the porch he took her in his arms.

"Don't grieve, Emma. I hate to see you unhappy, and Aunt Jessica would, too. Not your style," he added lightly.

Then he kissed her and her arms went round his shoulders, held him close, feeling the comfort and strength of him, before she whispered "Good-night," and slipped away.

Alone in her bedroom, she opened Miss Arlingham's letter.

My dear Emma,

I feel my time is short and, in case I am given no opportunity at the end, I am leaving this note to thank you for all you have done for me this past year, far, far beyond your duties as my employee. Your lively, intelligent mind and bright presence have made this one of the happiest and most fruitful years I have known for a long time. An old and often, I fear, irascible lady is not, one would think, a good companion for a young girl, yet we have been very good companions, and for that your kind heart and generous spirit must take the credit.

I hope life will deal kindly with you, dear Emma. I know that you will always meet its challenges bravely.

Your affectionate friend,
Jessica Arlingham.

It took Emma some weeks of hard work to complete *No Sad Songs*, despatch it to the publishers and sort out with Philip the vast quantity of papers, letters and documents left by Miss Arlingham, so that it was not until early in October that she drove over to Jean's cottage on a day of squally showers and high winds. The long, hot summer had broken with the advent of autumn and the grass in the meadows was green once more. She was looking forward to an hour or two with Jean, a relaxing person to be with, like a deep, calm pool after the turbulent waters of the past weeks.

Leaves scurried before her in the wind as she approached the cottage down the narrow lane. She drew up and stared, wondering for a moment if she had stopped at the wrong cottage. By the gate stood a 'For Sale' board and there was a closed deserted look about the place. She pushed open the gate and walked up the path to peer through the window of the sitting-room. It was bare of curtains and empty of furniture.

Bewildered, she drove slowly back to Broomfield. The pressure of work on *No Sad Songs*, followed by Miss Arlingham's death and all that had followed, had prevented her from seeing Jean for many weeks and, beyond a few words of condolence from Jean on the telephone at the loss of Jessica Arlingham, they had not been in touch.

Arriving back, Emma expressed her amazement to Mrs Bartlow.

"I can't understand it. My friend disappearing like this without a word."

The housekeeper put her hand to her mouth, dismayed.

"Oh, what's come over me? I've gone quite off the rails since the dear missis died. I remember now. Mrs Brynton telephoned one day when you were out. About a week or so after the funeral, I seem to recollect. Said would you ring her back? I clean forgot. I'd been sorting out Miss Arlingham's clothes and was a bit upset. It comes back to me now. I'm sorry, Emma."

"Not to worry. I'll hear in due course."

But she fretted about it during a restless night. Weeks had elapsed since that telephone call when Jean could have contacted her. It just wasn't like her to do anything precipitate, to vanish without a word.

The very next morning, however, brought a letter.

Dear Emma,

    At last I have a chance to write to you after the breathless whirl of the past few weeks.

    Nick and I were married very quietly three weeks ago. I tried to get in touch with you before I left the cottage, but no luck. It was at the time of Miss Arlingham's death and not opportune. Since then, we have been fully occupied getting Nick's house in the Cotswolds renovated and decorated to our liking, and seeing Diana settled into a new school for the autumn term. We are lucky to have a very good school not too far away – she will board during the week and come home at weekends, as it is a bit too far for daily journeys. She has taken to it happily.

    We returned yesterday from a short, belated honeymoon in Tuscany.

    Diana, needless to say, is delighted to have Nick for a father instead of a godfather!

This house is a gem, and I have to pinch myself sometimes to confirm that it is not all a dream. I had not thought to know such happiness again.

We hope you'll visit us before long. What are your plans now that your job at Broomfield has come to an end? Do keep us posted.

Our love to you.

Jean.

Emma read this through twice. From the somewhat jerky nature of the letter and its lack of detail, Emma guessed that Jean had not found it an easy letter to write. After all, writing to a friend to say you had married the man she was in love with was a little awkward, and although nothing explicit had passed between them on the subject, Jean was far too sensitive a person not to have sensed Emma's feelings.

Well, that was that, thought Emma, amazement more than grief uppermost in her mind. She expressed that amazement to Philip when she showed him the letter that evening.

He studied her closely as he handed it back, saying, "I don't know that it's so surprising."

"I just never imagined Jean marrying again. She seemed so settled somehow into a single life. So quiet. It never occurred to me . . ."

"She's still a young woman. She and Nick have been good friends for years, I believe."

"Yes. They have mutual interests. Both artistic. I suppose I've been very blind."

"Does it mean so much to you? Losing Nick, I mean?"

"I never had him. No, it doesn't shatter me. Nothing like it. I'm just sorry that I've lost two more friends to the closed shop of marriage."

"Not necessarily. They'll still be your friends, I'm sure."

"On the fringe, perhaps. But shut out, really. Anyway, Jean's a dear, and deserves her good fortune. She's sometimes seemed a sad and lonely person. Nick will do wonders for her. I guess he'll be in hot water with his family again, though, keeping it all so dark. I wonder what Auntie Barbie will say. I thought of going home next weekend, Phil, if that's all right by you? I've cleared up everything now."

"Of course. A couple of weeks in the Border country will be a tonic for you."

"Will you want me back? There's not much more I can do, except correct the proofs of the book when they come. That won't be for some time, though. Unless you want me to set about selling Broomfield?"

"Haven't decided anything yet. We'll discuss it when you get back. What about your commitments at the donkey sanctuary?"

"Jill's giving up the riding lessons, selling the horses and concentrating on looking after the existing donkeys. She won't be taking any more. That's all she can afford now. My disabled children are going to the Brushford Riding School. I'm sorry about that. I enjoyed teaching them."

"Yes. You were very good with them. Well, a break will do us both good. I'm attending a conference in Brussels next week, and may stay on for a few days. There's an exhibition of nineteenth-century paintings I'd like to go to."

"Will that interest Monica Ringford?" Emma asked blandly.

"Yes. She has her eye on one of the oil paintings for a client."

"And will be glad of your support, no doubt," said Emma, deciding that it was vinegar, not blood, in her veins.

"Monica, believe me, needs no support. You don't take to her, I fancy?"

He looked amused as she said, with a sparkle in her eyes, "I hardly know the lady and have no wish to spoil my good fortune."

"Dear Emma," he said laughing, "it's quite a time since I saw the light of battle in your eyes. I've quite missed it. Now I must be off. Have a good holiday and remember me to your parents."

He seemed to be in very good spirits, she thought darkly as she watched him drive off. Looking forward to a few days with that feline woman, no doubt. And somehow, as the sound of the car died away down the lane, it felt like the final desertion, and the worst one of all.

18

Happy Birthday

Emma had climbed to the top of the hill behind her home and now spread her windcheater on the grass at the foot of a mountain ash tree and sat down to enjoy the view, leaving the two retrievers to go off on their explorations. After a week of changeable weather, the sun was shining out of a pale blue sky that morning, enhancing the colours of autumn stretched before her, a tapestry of gold and green leaves, fading purple heather, russet brown bracken. The hills in the distance had a blue tinge about them. Below her, a twisting belt of dark green bushes and trees marked the course of a stream where she had seen a kingfisher the previous day.

Floss, soon tired, came back and stretched out beside her. Patting her and being thanked by a thump of her tail, Emma leaned back against the trunk of the tree reflecting on the year that had passed since her birthday a year ago exactly, and thought of the opening sentence of her favourite Dickens novel: 'It was the best of times, it was the worst of times.' The heady joy of falling in love with Nick, the barren result. The frustrating of her plans to have a business of her own with Lucy, and the loss of Lucy to Robert. The pleasure of Jean's friendship, and the loss of Jean to Nick. The rewarding work and friendship of her employer, now lost. And the imminent loss of her newly found friendship with Philip completing the same melancholy pattern. Everything seemed to have come to a dead end. A mood of desolation had swamped her this week and the efforts of hiding this from her family and putting on a bright face for the birthday celebrations planned for her had drained her. And somehow she had to face a party which Auntie Barbie was giving for her that evening and which normally she would have welcomed with joy. The south had rejected her, she thought, and her love for her own Border country had, for once, failed to comfort her.

Floss, as though sensing the melancholy mood of her mistress, moved up and rested her head on Emma's lap with a faint wag of her feathery tail. Stroking her by way of acknowledgment, Emma pondered on the enormous gap which severance from Philip would open up in her life. He had been such a thorn in her side and, although a somewhat volatile friendship had flowered over recent months, she was amazed at the hollow feeling inside her now at the thought of losing that friendship. Perhaps, she thought, thorns as well as flowers were a necessary part of the pattern.

She sighed and tried to summon up enough interest to continue her walk when Floss lifted her head and gave a little bark. Emma looked round, then sprang to her feet.

"Hullo, there!" called Philip.

She ran to meet him, her face radiant, and flung herself into his arms. Then, half embarrassed, drew back, but he drew her close again and kissed her.

"Happy birthday, Emma."

"How? When?"

"I'll join you under the tree. I'm not as fit as I ought to be. That hill has puffed me," he said, as they settled themselves on the grass.

"It is quite steep. Oh, it's so good to see you, Phil! When did you arrive?"

"Late last night. I'm staying at the Stag's Head in the village. Your mother thought I'd find you here."

"Oh, you could have stayed with us. How long are you here for?"

"A week. Don't want to use your home as a hotel. You promised to show me some walks up here, remember?"

"Yes."

145

"Your mother asked me if I knew if anything was wrong. She thinks you're unhappy. Are you?"

"Yes, I have felt rather low this week," said Emma, thinking that was the understatement of the year.

"Why? Is it because of Nick?"

"Nick? No, not particularly. It's just that, looking back on the year, I've found such good friends, only to lose them all now. Nick and Jean, Miss Arlingham, Lucy and now, with my job ending, you."

She was tugging at a piece of heather, head bent. He turned her towards him and cupped her face between his hands, then kissed her gently.

"I hadn't meant to say anything yet. Wasn't sure of the ground. But the warm welcome you gave me just now encourages me. I don't know how deeply you're still committed to Nick and I don't want to catch you on the rebound, but I love you, Emma. Once or twice lately, I've felt that you were beginning to care for me. Am I mistaken?"

"No."

"Then will you marry me?"

"We've fought a lot, Phil. Still would sometimes. You often exasperate me, you know."

"Yes, I do know," he said, smiling. "I don't think we should do each other lasting damage. You're far too volatile a person to live a placid life. I don't want to rush you, though. Will you think about it? I believe we could be happy together."

"You know, you've really surprised me, Phil. Oh, I know we've become good friends lately but I never thought you took me that seriously. Lucy had you more or less lined up with Monica Ringford, and I half thought as much."

"Monica and I are very old friends. I come in handy for an escort now and again, but we'd both run a mile from any prospect except the purely platonic. Her un-platonic needs are catered for elsewhere. I've never enquired into those. She abhors the very idea of marriage. And Monica, though likeable, is also unlovable. Trust Lucy to get such a potty idea."

"Then how long have you had this amazing idea about me?"

"I can tell you precisely. When I was last up here, at your Auntie Barbie's party. I was watching you dance the Gay Gordons. And my life was changed completely from that moment. But you haven't answered my question. Will you think about it, Emma darling? I do love you dearly."

"I have thought about it now. Although in some ways it seems a startling idea, I can't bear the thought of my life without you in it. That's really why I've been so unhappy this week. So yes, Phil. But isn't it incredible that I should have come to love you?"

And at this ingenuous remark, Philip threw back his head and laughed. Emma ruffled his hair and shook him, but it was some moments before he returned to sobriety.

"Oh, Emma! My darling Emma," he gasped. "How ever our marriage turns out, it will never be boring."

They were in a close embrace when Candy galloped up, tongue lolling, and jumped all over them.

Thus it was that Emma's birthday party became an engagement party that evening, and her radiant spirits infected them all.

During that week of calm autumn weather she showed Philip more of the walks in the hills she loved, and it was not until the week drew to a close that they discussed their plans for the future.

"How does the idea of living at Broomfield appeal to you, Emma? It's too big for us, of course, but I don't like the idea of dismissing the Bartlows. It's been their home for many years. It occurred to me that you might like to go into partnership with Jill Sandgate and use part of the garden to extend the sanctuary. We can easily spare the adjoining meadow. I'll help put in some capital and you can get it on to a sound, businesslike footing."

"What a splendid idea! I can throw my legacy in, too. I'm sure Jill will jump at it."

"And you can develop it. Take over the administration and use one of the rooms in the house for an office. It all needs refurnishing and decorating. I'd never envisaged

147

keeping such a big place, but I think we'd be happy there."

"It won't be too big. A lovely family house, which is what it was in the past. You'd like a family, Phil?"

"My experience of family life hasn't been exactly reassuring, but with you, yes, if and when you wish."

"I always thought I wanted to stay free and independent, no ties. But seeing Miss Arlingham so lonely at the end and contrasting it with the clan at home, I think I'd like a family, too. Some time. Not too soon, though. We've plenty of time."

"That's a relief. I'd like a year or two to ourselves first."

"What a lot of exciting prospects before us!" said Emma, tucking her arm in his as they left the riverside path and branched off towards home.

19

Quartet

On a sunny morning in June, Jean and Nick were in the garden awaiting their guests, Nick sitting in the shade of a lilac tree, Jean dead-heading some roses nearby. Behind them, the Cotswold stone house warmed to a soft golden colour in the sunshine, and the small-paned windows sparkled. The pale pink flowers of a rambling rose reached to one of the two small gables. Ben, the West Highland terrier, was snapping at a bumble-bee foraging among some pinks.

Jean walked to the low boundary hedge and looked across the lane up which the car must come, then joined Nick on the seat.

"It's a bit soon for them, dear, unless they left Pembroke very early," said Nick, putting his magazine aside.

"I'm glad it's such a lovely day for them after such an unsettled week. It's nearly a year since I saw Emma. I wonder how she's taken to married life?"

"With her customary zest, I expect."

"Her letters have sounded happy. She seems to lead a very busy life."

"Such energy! I expect Philip can cope, though. I rather took to what little I saw of him."

"Yes. It will be good to see them again."

"Bursting into our peaceful retreat?" said Nick, eyeing her quizzically.

Jean shook her head, smiling, and made no reply. It had been her suggestion to invite Emma and Philip to break their journey home after a holiday in Wales and stay the

149

night, an invitation which had been welcomed warmly by Emma, but Nick had seemed a little guarded about it and she wondered if he anticipated any untoward ripples from this meeting with Emma, who had undoubtedly been in love with him. Not that he had ever mentioned this, nor would he, but he was far too sensitive and shrewd not to have been fully aware of it and had handled it expertly, sliding away, avoiding any embarrassment, making sure that Emma did not become embroiled. She herself had experienced a slight uneasiness that Emma had married Philip Rogart on the rebound, but the tone of Emma's letters had all but banished it. That Nick would handle any awkwardness that might arise with his usual charming, light diplomacy, she had no doubt.

But there was nothing to justify any qualms during that day of reunion. From the moment Emma stepped out of the car, a wide smile on her face, an enthusiastic hug for each of them, the mood of the day was happy and carefree.

Over pre-lunch drinks in the garden, Emma, bursting with news, held sway. There was a gypsy look about her that day, thought Jean, listening to her tale of activities in developing the donkey sanctuary with Jill Sandgate. She was wearing a full, gaily flowered skirt with a white blouse, her fair hair tied back with a bright scarf, circular gold ear-rings gleaming in the sun, an air of radiant vitality about her. Philip, sipping his sherry, was content to sit back and watch his wife with indulgent eyes. There was no doubting their happiness. And that made four of them, thought Jean, her eyes meeting the lazy grey eyes of Nick and the ghost of a smile at his lips as though to say to her, "What did I tell you? Bursting into our peaceful retreat with all this verve."

Seeing the two young people, she was reminded of the heady early stages of her marriage to Darrel. Emma and Philip were at the May-time stage of love, she and Nick at late summer, the two halves of their love quartet very different in tempo and mood. Not for her and Nick the passionate heights and rocky hazards, but deep affection and untroubled companionship. But for her it had been nothing short of a resurrection. Since Darrel had been killed in the road accident, she had been half-petrified as an individual, merely existing to give Diana, his daughter, as good a home as she could, expecting nothing, willing nothing for herself. She had never entertained the thought of marriage again. Could never have married anybody to whom Darrel Brynton was just a name. But Nick had been his friend too, had known them both from the beginning of their courtship, and she knew that Darrel would approve of their union. As for Philip and Emma, they had it all to make, but the foundations looked promising to her.

Emma's laugh rang out at some quip of Nick's which she had missed.

"What cool nerve! No sign of repentance. You don't deserve to be forgiven. Marrying secretly without telling any of your friends or relations, then failing to come to our wedding."

"My dear girl, I was buried shoulder deep in the dusty archives of an Italian museum at the time, having had some difficulty in getting permission to ransack them."

"No excuse. And heart-rending appeals from Auntie Barbie to get you to Foresters for Christmas, then Easter, getting no result. You don't deserve your sister."

"True enough, but remember Shakespeare's observation: 'Use every man after his desert, and who would 'scape whipping?'"

"Well, in case you've forgotten what your Northumberland relatives look like, I've brought you a photograph taken at our wedding which includes the lot of them and us."

"That will be treasured," said Nick gravely.

"You're incorrigible. I don't know why we go on wanting to see you."

"No doubt because you see so little of me. Distance lends enchantment, as you know."

"I think you're dead clever at organising your life just as you want it."

"You can't blame me for that, and I'm not always successful. But I admit that I'm fortunate beyond my deserts, not least in Jean, who puts up with my regrettable

151

ways with exemplary kindness and forbearance. I doubt whether you'll let Philip off so lightly."

"My shoulders are broad," said Philip, smiling.

"He has methods which, in his own way, are as effective as yours, Nick," said Emma.

"Well, well, that must add up to a very interesting state of affairs. Jean and I must seem like a couple of fossils in this quiet backwater," observed Nick, his eyes teasing Emma, who said feelingly, "Some fossils!"

"Well, I must try to soften your harsh criticism by telling you that I have promised my sister that Jean, Diana and I will spend a week with her in early September before Diana goes back to school. Jean and Diana shall experience for themselves that rugged country before the rigours of the northern winter set in. Any mountaineering I shall leave to them."

And before Nick and Emma could embark on the north versus south contest, Jean ushered them into lunch.

After a leisurely walk that afternoon along the winding path that led to the village, they were all ready to relax with some music as the sun began to sink.

Emma, the least knowledgeable of the four of them, but with an uncritical enjoyment of music generally, leaned back in an armchair with Ben, who had taken a fancy to her, curled up on her lap, and found her thoughts wandering against a background of Bach, a composer always liable to send her concentration sliding away like water over a weir. Stroking Ben's tousled white head, she reflected on the day with satisfaction. No aches at seeing Nick again. Or perhaps a very tiny one, deep down. But she realised now that she would never have fitted into his ivory tower. She would always admire him, enjoy his company and know virtually nothing of the man beneath the urbane exterior.

She looked across the room at the two men in her life. The contrast between them could hardly be greater. Nick, slim, elegant, leaning back, eyes veiled, deep in the music. He was wearing a lightweight silver-grey jacket and trousers with a pale blue shirt and flowing royal blue and gold striped tie, his fair hair shining in the light of a standard lamp nearby, his classical profile clearly defined against the dark upholstery of the chair. He possessed a charisma for her that she had found irresistible and still enjoyed, knowing that in hoping to get close to him she had grasped air.

Close by, Philip, dark, tanned after their holiday, tall and strongly built, gave an impression of rugged force beside Nick's cool elegance. In navy trousers and a white cotton roll top sweater, he looked lean and stripped for action. She had sensed that he had not been altogether enthusiastic about this visit but he appeared to have enjoyed it and was now absorbed in Bach. And, after only six months, she could not envisage life without him. Her eyes had turned back to Nick, and she was wondering whether she could leave it to him to give her a copy of his new book or whether she should drop a hint, when she shifted in her chair to re-settle Ben and caught her husband's eyes on her. He looked . . . she could not quite define it. Pain was there, or was it a trick of the subdued light and the shadows in the room as the Brandenburg Concerto came to an end?

And that night he made love to her with an urgency that suggested that she had not been mistaken, and that doubts were plaguing him about her feelings towards Nick. Afterwards, with his head on her breast, her fingers moving gently in his hair, she knew he would not question her and ached to reassure him, but found it difficult to frame words which would do so.

They left soon after breakfast the next morning and made good time for the first half of the journey, then ran into heavy traffic and one bad hold-up caused by an accident, so that it was late afternoon before they arrived back at Broomfield.

Dumping their suitcases in the hall and picking up the post, Philip said, "Down to earth again. Back to the workaday world."

"That's where we belong. Both of us, Phil."

"So we do," he said with a little smile and went to pick up the suitcases again.

"Leave them, Phil. Let's have a cup of tea first. You need it after all that driving."

153

While Emma disappeared to the kitchen, Philip opened up the windows of the sitting-room and stood gazing out of the window, reflecting on the past twenty-four hours. He wondered whether Emma had ever sensed the streak of pessimism beneath Nick's wit and charm, his distaste of the era he lived in and his rejection of it. "The barbarians are at the gate," he had said to Philip during their walk along the river. Emma had a totally different attitude to life, her hands open to it, eager to embrace it, sure that it was good. That was what he most loved about her. But Nick, he thought, still attracted her. Or was he letting jealousy creep in and blind him? So easy to be possessive when you loved someone as he loved Emma. He turned as she came in.

"Tea up," she said cheerfully. "You look tired to death, Phil."

She looked at him, then put the tray down and joined him at the window. Tucking her hand under his arm, she said, "It's good to be home, isn't it? Just us, together, where we belong. I love you, Phil. Only you. Now and for ever. You must know that."

And when he caught her to him, she could see from his deeply moved expression that this reassurance was what he had long been waiting and hoping for. He held her closely and was without words for a few moments, then said in a faintly unsteady voice, "That's all that matters to me."